My Friend Pasquale and Other Stories

James Selwin Tait

Table of Contents

CHAPTER I.

THE events narrated in the following story happened a score and more of years ago. They have never before been made public, and I make them known now with pain and misgiving, but impelled by a sense of duty which I can no longer disregard.

During their occurrence they changed the current of my life, once from grave to gay, and then and finally, from gaiety to unspeakable gloom. Although time has to some extent dulled the edge of my grief at the loss of my friend Pasquale, his memory will remain with me while life lasts as a cherished and sacred thing.

When the reader ends this simple narration this eulogy of the dead may surprise and shock him, and, in reply and explanation, I have only to say in advance that I pity him if the faithful, unvarnished record leaves that impression on his mind— he did not know Pasquale.

I was wending my way homeward from Hampstead Heath one Saturday afternoon in the early summer time, when I found myself, on recovering from a lengthened reverie, midway on the Old North Road at a point now occupied by the Midland Railway Terminus at Saint Pancras.

My day's work at the bank was finished and with it all the duties of the week, and I felt that sense of relief and buoyancy which, perhaps, comes to all, young and old alike, at the completion of tedious work honestly performed.

I was still—at the period of which I write—a good deal of a day-dreamer, living in a world of my own for many hours of the twenty-four, and when the heavy bank doors clanged behind me, with all business cares and anxieties doubly barred within the impregnable vault, my mind would soar away from business thoughts as an imprisoned lark leaps to freedom from its narrow cage.

The road I was traveling was not one which I would have

taken intentionally, but in my fit of absent-mindedness I had unconsciously followed the trend of the highway with the result that I was committed to one of the most uninviting thoroughfares in the city of London.

As a highway this road was but little used; it had already been secured by the railway company, and with the exception of one public-house of low character there were no dwellings fronting it, but only the wreck of the torn down structures demolished to make way for the company's projected improvements; and this wreckage was walled, or penned in, by a high and closely boarded fence running the full length of the road.

The Old North Road was nearly a mile in length between these wooden walls, and it was a street to be shunned not only by females but by solitary travelers of even the stronger sex, for it afforded no means of escape from an unpleasant encounter.

When I had traveled about one third of its length my attention was attracted to an excited group of men some three hundred yards distant.

These men I found, on nearing them, to be coal-heavers employed by the railway company, and already a good deal exhilarated by their wages-day libations.

They were broad-shouldered, powerful men—a collection of sooty giants—and the sport which they were enjoying was an impromptu dog-fight, an amusement entirely after their own heart.

As I approached the group on the one side, a young man of about my own age neared it from the other, and we both stopped to ascertain the cause of the excitement.

The sight of one dog apparently killing the other was to me a revolting spectacle, and I was turning away in disgust when I saw the other arrival elbow his way fiercely through the men and attempt to drag off the dog which seemed to be gaining the victory; in doing which he certainly risked his life.

"O, you great, black cowards!" he shouted, his voice ringing in the air like a trumpet, "to allow two poor creatures to worry each other in such a way!"

His movements were so sudden that he had actually grasped one of the dogs before his intention could be frustrated, but as soon as he touched the animal a burly coal-heaver seized him round the waist, and lifting him high in air, carried him out of the crush into the middle of the road, where he planted him on the ground and released his hold. Not ill-naturedly altogether, but yet with a warning look in his grimy face he placed his bulky body in front of the disturber of the fight, saying as he did so, "Master, we are not molesting you, leave us alone, or — —" the threat in his eyes supplied the rest.

The stranger whose face was pale as death, and whose eyes literally flamed with rage, said not a word, but, quick as lightning, his right hand shot out and struck his opponent straight between the eyes. The amazing fury of the blow, the skill with which it was given, and the smallness of the hand which struck it, had, to some extent, the same effect on the dense skull of the coal-heaver as the pole axe has on the head of the ox. He fell, not backward, but forward, on his knees, as a bullock falls when struck.

The group around the two dogs had given no more thought to the intruder after their companion had removed him, but now one looked around and seeing his friend on the ground and probably concluding that the foreign-looking stranger had stabbed him, he rushed to secure the intruder.

The latter, however, seemed possessed with an ungovernable fury and flew at his new assailant as if he would rend him to pieces. Even a blow from the ponderous fist, though it landed him three yards away flat on his back in the dusty road, in nowise discouraged him. In a moment he was on his feet flying like a tiger-cat at his antagonist's throat, his dark eyes gleaming anew with electric fire. In the midst of the *mêlée* a hansom cab drove up, and the driver stopped to witness the double event.

Others of the group now gathered around, and I feared, not for the safety of the stranger's limbs, but for his life. It was an "ugly" group for any single man to attack. These men, although easygoing enough up to a certain point, were incarnate fiends when roused, and they were already disposed to be quarrelsome.

At length the coal-heaver tore the other from his throat, and getting him at arm's length promptly felled him to the ground.

No movement this time—was he dead? That sledge-hammer blow might well have fractured the skull of a delicate man!

Such men don't always stop at knock-down blows, and when one, the worse for liquor, shouted "Kill the fellow," I called to the cabman, "For Heaven's sake get the injured man out of this." "You get him inside here," promptly replied the driver. "Stand back!" I yelled to the men with a horrified air, which was only half-assumed; "you have killed him," and stooping down I raised the slender figure in my arms. As I did so the cabman turned his horse as if to drive off, but in reality in order to put his vehicle between the men and myself. This he did with much adroitness and without obstruction, as the others thought he was simply preparing to leave.

His movement enabled me to place the slowly recovering figure in the hansom cab without interference.

"Drive on!" I shouted, but, alas! a smoke-colored Hercules had seen my movements and had grasped the horse's head with a grip of iron. It was the brute who had yelled "Kill him."

Knowing remonstrance to be entirely useless I struck the wretch with my stick with all the force I could muster. He staggered under the blow and released his hold. A moment more and the horse sprang forward, and as the cab passed me I caught at the driver's seat, and with one hand on that and a foot on the powerful spring which supported the body of the carriage on that side, I managed to hold on until we were clear of the dangers which threatened us.

When I joined my fellow-traveler inside the cab, I found him crouching on his knees with his head buried in the cushion of the seat. He had recovered consciousness and was moaning softly.

"Are you hurt?" I inquired as I entered the cab, alarmed lest the merciless blow of the laborer should have done the stranger some serious injury.

The face which was upturned to my gaze was ghastly pale, and a wide semi-circle of sombre shadow under the dark weird-looking eyes lent to the latter a strange unnatural brilliancy.

"No, I am not hurt," he replied; "but it always upsets me very much to witness cruelty of any kind: did you see the dogs?"

As he made the inquiry a shudder ran through his frame as if the recollection of the sickening spectacle had revolted him anew.

The rest of the journey to my quarters was performed in silence, while I, mindful of the mad fury of my companion's attack on the coal-giant, labored mentally to discover where the consistency lay in trying to seriously injure a human being because he objected to the stoppage of a dog-fight. I had, indeed, no love for the brutal coal-heaver, but I was nevertheless sensible of a spirit of incongruity about my companion's actions, and I was still puzzling over the problem when the cab reached its destination—my own rooms.

After I had assisted my fellow-traveler to alight, and had discharged my obligations to the cabman, the latter, addressing my new friend, told him that he had undoubtedly had a narrow escape. "Had those men got hold of you at the last, a squad of police could not have saved you; you have to thank that gentleman that you are not now lying battered out of shape on the Old North Road; and I know both the men and the place."

When the stranger heard this he turned towards me with eyes suffused with tears, and raised my hand to his lips.

"I thank you for saving my life," he murmured, "and I will never forget the debt I owe you."

I replied, somewhat ashamed at the novel attention I was receiving, that but for the cabman the incident on the road would probably have proved fatal to both of us.

When the cabman left he carried with him a *pour-boir* which made the compensation paid by myself mean and contemptible in comparison.

"Thank'ee, sir, and God bless'ee. If ever either of ye want a friend I hope Will Owen may be on hand to take the office;" saying which he wheeled his cab as on a pivot, saluted with the handle of his whip, touched his horse with the lash, and drove off.

When I turned to my companion I found him staring confusedly at the houses.

"Why—where are we?" he inquired with considerable astonishment in his voice.

"In Russell Square, and this is where I live," pointing to No. 12, where the hansom had stopped.

"Well, that is certainly very remarkable," he observed with a low laugh of astonishment. "Why, I live next door to you." Saying this he handed me his card, on which I found engraved, Amidio Pasquale, 13 Russell Square, London. "I chose No. 13 for a residence to see whether there were any ill-luck in the number." This last remark was the result of my having somewhat unconsciously repeated the word "thirteen;" but I was thinking only of the extraordinary coincidence that we who had been brought together under such circumstances that day as would almost certainly tend to bind us to each other in future, should find ourselves already next-door neighbors.

Was it a coincidence—or was it only the first distinct move made by the finger of fate on the chess-board of our lives?

Now, in these later years, when I recall the terrible ending to our brief friendship begun that afternoon, it seems to my embittered and discouraged soul that there was naught of coincidence in the circumstance at all but, that, the time having come, Destiny began her grim and blood-stained task in that kindly work of mercy attempted on the Old North Road that day, reckless whether the blows which fell so unrelentingly from her hand were struck by means of the crosier of the Churchman or by the bludgeon of the assassin; or whether it was the pinion of an angel or the hoof of a demon which she had seized to speed her in her dire inscrutable work.

Is it because Man's best deeds fall so far short of the approval of the Immortal Gods that ofttimes they appear to be used—in sheer satire—as instruments of untold misery and tragedy?

My friend accompanied me to my rooms, and for a time he sat in silence, crouching over the fire in the grate, and every now and then shivering as if from the sight of another horror.

"Did the appearance of the dogs impress you so very painfully?" I inquired, anxious to find some solution for my new friend's state of semi-hysteria.

"O don't speak of it!" he exclaimed, his voice quivering with emotion, and the tears welling in his eyes, "One dog was literally being worried to death!"

"O yes," I replied, "it looks like that, but there are many ups and downs even in a dog fight; probably the under dog had its turn after a while, and it is surprising how much chewing they can stand from each other and be but little the worse."

Pasquale turned upon me speechless for the moment with horror. Then, ere his glance had lengthened to a stony glare, he said with an apparent effort at restraint, "But I forgot you did not see the animals, and cannot therefore know how terrible it all was."

"Well, be content," I hastened to say by way of encouragement. "You did your best; you knocked one coal-heaver almost senseless, and you tore the other's neck-tie to pieces, besides lacerating his face, and——"

"Do you know," he interrupted, striding up to me with his eyes aflame and the veins standing out round and black on his forehead, "do you know, sir, that I would have liked to tear those men limb from limb for stopping me, and I almost think I would have done so, if I had not been prevented."

And I thought so too, as I gazed at him standing there almost suffocated with the fury of passion.

This strange anomaly—this combination of dove-like tenderness, and tigerish ferocity was a complete mystery to me, and I felt bewildered at the contemplation of it.

After a time my friend's mood changed, and he apologized humbly for his outbreak. "I am entirely unhinged by the events of the day," he said gently. "I am not usually like this, I can assure you"—a statement fully borne out by my after-experience of him, for a brighter, gentler, more delightful companion I shall never again meet in this world.

His last words as he left me were: "I am not feeling well, and shall go away for a week, but when I return you and I must see much of each other."

CHAPTER II.

LIFE in London had great attractions for me during the first year of my residence in that wonderful city. Not because of the gaieties of the metropolis, for of those I knew nothing, while of its more solid attractions my ignorance was equally great.

So long as my books retained their charms I had no appetite for other recreations or attractions.

The busy crowds which in my homeward journey pressed past me on all sides, callous as to my welfare and heedless of my existence, delighted me because they gave me, with a sensation which thrilled me like a passion, the enchantment of an isolation and seclusion greater than those of the unpeopled desert.

When I arrived at home I gave myself up unreservedly to the enjoyment of my library.

My rooms were comfortably and even richly furnished, and the apartments themselves were of imposing dimensions. Before the tide of fashion had rolled westward from Russell Square, the house in which I lived had been a mansion of considerable pretensions; and this, to suit the more modest requirements of the new class of tenants now occupying the square, had been divided into two good-sized houses.

The cutting of the house in two had resulted oddly at some points, and in my rooms signs of new walls, foreign to the original design of the building, were discernible; as were also two massive oaken doorways which had apparently at one time communicated with the opposite house, but had since been closed up.

Of these two doors more hereafter.

The bright fire, the softly-shaded light, the dainty surroundings and the book I loved, suggested something of a Sybaritish existence during my evenings, and sometimes my conscience pricked me about yielding so unreservedly to what certainly was a most pleasant enjoyment.

I need not, however, have fretted at the slender

dissipation, since the hour was already on the wing which was to shatter the repose of my life into fragments, and to tarnish for evermore the gold with which these earlier days were being perhaps over-gilded.

Life, however pleasant, had seemed tame beside the dramas of Literature; soon Fiction was to pale before the tragedies of Fact.

Pasquale called upon me immediately on his return, and as I found him then he continued without change until the end. Bright, cheery, brilliant and debonair, his sun suffered no eclipse until it sank forever.

Our acquaintance soon ripened into the warmest friendship, and ere long the wonderful charm of his manner began to wean me from the books which had hitherto enslaved me.

When at no lengthy intervals he came to "rout me out" and carry me off for a long walk through the crowded streets I closed my volume with ever lessening regret.

His powers of perception, naturally great, had been trained until they had all the acuteness of the most delicate sense, and allied to a mind accustomed to reason inductively they filled his brain with scenes lost to the ordinary observer.

At the first glance he seemed to penetrate the mask which disguised the true character of those he was brought in contact with. The various hand-writings which mark the human visage, as well as the influences which mould the actions of the body, seemed alike familiar to him, and when the pros and cons were duly weighed in his logical brain the real character of the individual, and not the outward pretence, lay mapped out before him with wonderful accuracy and promptness considering the inexactness of the science which he cultivated.

Hence it was that, to myself, wrapped up in my books and blind to the outer world, his analysis of the individuals who passed us in our nightly walks, seemed marvelous in the extreme.

Occasionally we went to the music halls, but I think that, catching the infection from my friend, I studied the onlookers rather than the somewhat offensive and vulgar display on the boards.

Truth to tell, I relished Pasquale's company a great deal more without such tawdry surroundings. It was at that time a source of considerable wonder to me what attraction my brilliant friend could find in my dull society, and I sometimes endured the passing and humiliating reflection that he simply used me as a species of human target into which he could shoot the sharp arrows of his fancy, or may be, as a very rough commonplace file against which to edge them.

Occasionally I called upon my friend by way of acknowledgment of his many visits to myself, but I must have been very unfortunate, for the answer given unhesitatingly was invariably: "Mr. Pasquale has gone out."

Once indeed his landlady, who was an American by birth, told the servant to go up to the third floor and see whether her lodger was in, but the answer received was the same—"He is not at home."

Strange to say, my friend, who was so communicative on impersonal topics, was so reticent about his own affairs, that this was the first intimation I had received as to the floor on which he lived.

"You live on the third floor, I live on the second," I remarked on the occasion of his next visit, anxious to furnish something new to the conversation.

"Indeed!" he remarked by way of reply, giving me, I fancied, a sharp glance and adding quickly, "How did you discover that, Wyndham?"

When I told him he smiled, and then added, "I go out a great deal. I love long walks and am quite unable to bury myself in books as you do, my friend; I wish you would come with me more frequently."

This implied-craving for my society was entirely unintelligible to me, for Pasquale's marvelous brightness and gaiety rendered my own stolidity more apparent to myself day by day. No discouragement seemed to daunt him, no business cares worried him. From the first moment that he joined me till he left, his language and his expression were radiant with humor and buoyant light-heartedness.

Of money troubles he had, or appeared to have, none, and he explained to me in a moment of exceptional confidence that his father, who was an Italian wine-grower, had sent him to London to learn the wine-business there, in order that he might eventually open a branch establishment in the English metropolis.

"I have no extravagant tastes," he added, "and my father is wealthy and generous, so that I am usually well in funds; so, Wyndham, if ever you are hard up, you must make me your banker."

Little by little this strange, bright creature woke me from my old-world dreams, until at length, for the first time since my arrival in London, I felt the evenings drag when he failed to put in an appearance. His sunny nature had become to me a panacea for all the dull and oppressive cares of my own life, and I craved for his company, in which nothing sordid or gloomy could live.

Pasquale, in spite of his apparently volatile nature, was a great reader of a certain class of books, as well as a close student of human nature, and now and again he would astonish me by his information on all questions touching the phenomena of mind and matter.

"My friend," he remarked one day, "you traverse all roads at intervals, and therefore cross the same parallels of thought again and again; I only travel one for the most part untrodden, and on that lonely and fearsome path I am leagues beyond your utmost thought and that of, I think, every other human being. In fact I imagine that I must be close to the pole of human search;

anyhow," he broke off merrily, "I feel cold enough for such a northern latitude, and am glad to warm myself by your beautiful fire."

Shortly after this I felt a great inclination for a moonlight sail on the Thames, and having received an invitation to join a boating party I asked permission to bring my friend.

"You have never seen the Thames by moonlight," I remarked to him, "and I am told that it is lovely beyond description. On Thursday next it will be full-moon; will you come?"

I had spoken warmly in my anxiety to secure his company, but he answered me coldly, "I cannot accompany you —I am full of sympathies and antipathies; I love you, Wyndham, as much, I think, as life itself, but I hate and loathe the moonlight worse than death. Don't stare at me, dear boy, it is constitutional and cannot be helped."

Rather than go alone or leave my friend I gave up the intended trip on the river, but for the next week I, nevertheless, saw nothing of him. He was reported "not at home." When he returned he informed me, in reply to my inquiry as to his absence, that he had been called out of town. He had often been absent in a similar way before and the occurrence occasioned me no surprise.

Shortly after this I was sent to the United States by the firm I represented, to deliver certain papers of importance to a client in Chicago.

As I was about to leave, my friend Pasquale somewhat surprised me by saying, "Wyndham, I can't stand this place without you, so I think I shall go off for a time too; my father has been urging me for a long while to take a two months' holiday, and has recommended Norway salmon-fishing as a soothing and pleasant recreation. Sport of the kind would be worse than death to me with my hatred of seeing suffering: so, as he leaves the choice to me, I am thinking of going over to Paris. I happen to know the Chief of Police there, and I want to master their wonderful detective system and to see whether I am right in supposing that I know more than others do about the peculiarities of the human mind, more especially in its relation to the perpetration of crime; and, so, dear old friend," he concluded, "if you hear of any wonderful captures during your absence, look out for my name!"

And so we parted with, on my side, many a yearning heartache for the friend I was leaving behind me.

As the stately Cunarder carrying me on board steamed out from Liverpool, the same day a channel boat bore Pasquale from Dover to Calais.

CHAPTER III.

WHEN I arrived in New York I had not much opportunity of reading up back numbers of the daily papers, but I was startled to see that the Chief Commissioner of the London Police, Sir Charles Pendreth, had been found dead in his bed by his own hand, and that, immediately following upon his suicide, had occurred that of two of the leading police magistrates of the metropolis.

These occurrences, dire enough in themselves, were rendered still more terrible by the fact that each had killed himself in the same way—by severing his jugular vein with his razor,—and had left behind him a letter in his well-known handwriting explaining why he had committed self-destruction.

In the case of the first suicide the coroner's jury had found considerable difficulty in avoiding a verdict of *felo-de-se*, as the letter left behind displayed so manifest a purpose; but in the other cases the deaths were unhesitatingly attributed to the spreading of an epidemic of suicide, and the verdict of temporary insanity rendered in both instances threw a merciful veil over the intentions of the self-slain.

On my return to New York from Chicago I found a letter awaiting me. It was from my friend Pasquale, and the sight of his handwriting thrilled me with joy. Heaven alone knew how dry and barren my life had seemed without him all these long weeks spent in dreary, uninteresting travel.

Pasquale stated in his letter that he had found his stay in Paris very agreeable (I winced jealously at the thought) and instructive, and that while there he had seen no reason to moderate his views as to his ability to unravel any criminal plot, or to account for any mental obliquity; and in virtue of this additional confidence in himself, and of the further experience which he had gained, he proposed to go to London shortly to endeavor to solve the mystery of the terrible mania for self-destruction in that city.

Pasquale's letter was dated the 1st of October; he hoped to arrive in London on the 31st. So did I. Thank God, my old friend and I would soon meet.

On the 1st of November the good ship "Saragossa" landed me safely in Liverpool, and at 7. P.M. the same evening my cab drove up to the door of No. 12 Russell Square.

As I descended from my cumbersome four-wheeler I noticed a hansom cab dash up to the adjoining house, and words would fail me to express the rapture with which I saw my friend alight.

His welcome was like a bath of electrified sunshine, so gay, so bright and thrilling was it in its *empressement*, and as soon as he had seen his portmanteau safely housed he turned to me, his whole voice vibrating with pleasure.

"Wyndham, I can't ask you into my dull quarters, but you and I must see much of each other to-night to make up for our long separation, so as soon as we have taken our baths and a chop I will run in to spend a couple of hours with you, and I've got some lovely French cognac which the occasion will absolve us for using,—dear, dear Wyndham, on my soul I'm glad to see you—" and before I could retreat, much to my embarrassment, he had clasped me by the shoulder and imprinted a hearty kiss, first on one cheek, and then on the other.

"I missed you more than tongue can tell," he continued, and as he spoke the tears in his voice made it husky, as the glad mist in my own eyes made my vision dim.

I noticed that Pasquale had brought back a French valet with him from Paris, a tall, muscular and rather forbidding man in appearance, with the stamp of the army or police about his square shoulders, stiff neck and mechanical step.

"An old army man," I murmured to myself; "an officer's servant, most likely."

"You are becoming somewhat more fastidious, my friend," I remarked, in reference to the valet.

"No, no, Wyndham," was the reply; "Jacques is supposed to be my valet, but he is in reality a detective to help me in the work of penetrating the English mystery. Sometimes one good clue becomes lost while you are hunting up another, and Jacques' duty will be to follow the scent before it grows cold, while I am doing something else; but, pray don't tell anyone about him."

What a delightful couple of hours we spent. As the clock struck eleven my friend rose to go. By that time he had given me a full history of his doings in Paris, and it would certainly have been difficult for a less enterprising individual to have managed to accomplish so much of actual work and positive enjoyment in so short a time.

"Then you never visited London at all during those two months?" I inquired.

"Not once," was the reply; "I should have hated to visit my old haunts while you were away."

With Pasquale back the old days returned, bringing with them the sunshine which seemed to crown him like a nimbus, and scatter its radiance all around.

As I stood by the old carved mantelpiece, winding up my watch after the door closed on him that evening, my heart was full of an exhilarating gaiety to which it had long been a stranger.

If I—a man by nature harsh and cold—regarded Pasquale with such tender feelings, what emotions must he arouse in the gentler sex, and what unutterable havoc must he work with their tender susceptibilities!

While this thought was exercising my brain, and as I turned into the inner room, I became conscious of a deep groan uttered on the opposite side of the blind doorway which stood between my bedroom and the room on the same floor in the adjoining house.

I recollected that Pasquale had informed me that the floor under him, that is, the one adjoining my rooms, was occupied by a troublesome old Frenchman whose peculiar ways gave the people of the house a good deal of trouble.

I waited for a time in silence, but the groan was not repeated, and, eventually, I retired to rest, and to enjoy an unbroken and dreamless sleep.

I awoke somewhat late the following morning, and as I was not obliged to report myself at the office at the usual hour on that occasion, and as I was, moreover, somewhat fatigued, I proposed to enjoy my breakfast in bed and my morning's newspaper as well—- to me an unprecedented luxury.

If I had anticipated that my morning meal should be enjoyed in comfort I was doomed to be disappointed, for I had scarcely tasted my food before a thundering knock at the door announced my friend Pasquale, who burst into my room newspaper in hand, and with outstretched finger pointed to the giant head lines on the newspaper, "Another Suicide—- Death of Inspector Reynolds by his own hand."

"Now, my friend, you will see whether my boasted skill is of any use. If I do not prove to your satisfaction that there is something more in these suicides than meets the eye, I will agree to forfeit everything in life."

I was thunderstruck and horrified. I pushed the paper away from me with the first trace of genuine impatience which I think I had ever displayed towards my friend.

"Take your horrid sheet away, Pasquale," I exclaimed, "I don't understand your ghoulish glee——," but my voice failed me when I saw the look of pain and remorse which crossed his face.

"Wyndham, I swear to you before God," he replied with an earnestness which it is pitiful to remember, "that I would not injure a hair of anyone's head whom the Good Lord has made, no, not for life itself, if I knew it."

My friend left shortly afterwards, cast down, it seemed to me, in spite of my reiterated assurance that I had spoken hastily and tetchily, having only just been waked out of my sleep.

When I returned to my apartments that evening there had been up to that time no indication of any clue to the cause of the suicide, beyond the strange, unsatisfactory letter which, as in the other cases of suicide, had been left behind him by the dead man; and the condition of the public mind was, in consequence, one of profound horror and anxiety.

I had hardly dared to hope that my friend Pasquale would forget the hastiness of my morning's greeting so far as to call upon me, and I was accordingly relieved beyond measure when I heard the old familiar knock.

He came in—with at first a glance askance—almost of timidity, such a glance as a loving, warm-hearted woman might give to an offended and over-sensitive friend. When he noticed my shamefacedness he advanced gracefully towards me with outstretched hands, looking altogether too pretty a picture to waste on a cold-blooded stiff-mannered Briton, and added hugely to my embarrassment by kissing me softly on either cheek.

That terrible foreign fashion—would I ever get accustomed to it! "Thank God! Wyndham, you and I are all right! If we were to quarrel I should give everything up in despair."

The evening passed as a hundred others had gone before it; in controversy, brilliant and conclusive on the one side, and stupid and dogmatic on the other.

"Your obstinacy almost converts me, it is so magnificent, in its contempt of law and fact."

Such was the Parthian shaft which Pasquale launched as he bowed himself out, genial and smiling, as if our every sentence had been a harmonious duet; but the parting words rankled in my sensitive breast, and as the door closed behind my friend, I sat still and silent in a cold defiant mood.

"Good-night, old friend," said a soft and musical voice at my elbow. "Forgive my banter; I won't sleep a wink if you don't shake hands with me."

Pasquale had softly re-entered the room and stood gazing at me with a tender wistful look.

I gave him my hand somewhat grudgingly,—it pains me to remember,—and after one glance at the pathetic eyes I resumed my stare at the dying embers.

Oh, memory! Oh, days and years that have been! how much more bitter than death itself are your whisperings of lost opportunities, of loving deeds undone, loving words unsaid, of loving glances withheld!

After Pasquale had gone I sat for a while reflecting on what he had told me about the result of his preliminary investigations into the cause of the epidemic of suicide which was paralyzing the entire city.

One peculiar feature of these horrors he had especially dwelt upon—namely, the fact that in each case the suicide had left a letter stating that he had determined to take his own life. As to the authenticity of these letters the authorities appeared to have no doubt whatever. On comparison with other specimens of the dead men's handwriting they could not, it was declared, be called in question.

Then, too, there was the extraordinary similarity as to method. Each man had, with great deliberation, severed his jugular vein, using for the purpose his own razor, which, in every instance, had been found firmly clasped in the right hand of the suicide.

"The Press call it a contagion of suicide," Pasquale had said, with a smile of contempt which had roused my easily stirred ire, "now I say it is nothing of the kind. It is murder and not suicide, and I will prove it so."

Yes, that had been the absurdly egotistical remark which had finally exhausted my forbearance. I had no patience with such hair-brained ideas.

During the next week I saw nothing of my volatile friend,

and when he finally made his appearance he looked pale and, I imagined, thinner.

"I have been called away," he explained to me during this visit, "and I must now redouble my efforts to work out my theory as to those so-called suicides."

On the next occasion when he visited my rooms he told me with great exultation that he had at length received from a prominent expert in handwriting the assurance, after a searching examination, that the letters purporting to have been written by the poor suicides had all been penned by the same hand; and that on careful comparison, although wonderful forgeries, they were all essentially different in character from the handwritings of the dead men.

"Such is the opinion of the expert I employed," continued Pasquale, "but looking to the gravity of the subject and the responsibility of making so serious a statement, before handing his written report to me he has taken the precaution to obtain the opinion of two other experts on the subject. These opinions," continued my friend with something of the exultation which had previously repelled me, "entirely endorse the views of the expert which I employed."

When Pasquale produced the letter received from his expert, I found that his statement had in nowise been exaggerated. The original view and the opinions endorsing it, written in cold and well-weighed language, rested in my hand for a moment; then I dropped the dread papers on the table as I would have thrown from my grasp a cluster of poisonous reptiles.

I was horrified, and expressed myself so. I had never before, it seemed to me, been in such proximity to crime, and I shuddered at the contact with this terrible link.

"And that is not all," resumed my friend, "the death wounds were not made by the razors grasped in the hands of the dead men, or at least not in the case of the last victim, for, unfortunately, the bodies of the others have been interred and I have not been able to examine them.

"A razor cuts with a slash or gash, but it does not and cannot make a stab, whereas in the last case there was, first of all, a stab penetrating far into the neck, and that was followed by a long cut which severed the great artery and all the surrounding flesh. That is to say, the murderer thrust the knife into the neck, then drew it towards himself, and then the deed was complete."

As my friend spoke, carried away by his subject apparently and insensible to its revolting character, I grew dumb, petrified with the horror of his revelations. His eyes, always brilliant, shone large and clear and seemed to stand out from the pale ivory features. There was in his appearance the force and pride of elucidation which a successful counsel might show in entangling the criminal in the noose destined to terminate his existence; but there was more than that: there was the physical and mental ardor of the chase, and the flash of eye and teeth which the Zulu Caffre shows when he poises his willing spear to flesh it in his human victims.

"And do you know," he went on, while I grew sick and giddy beneath the horror of his narration, and the uncanny mesmerism of his eyes, "the murderer, whoever he was, must, after all, have been a bungler, for, just think of it, would any man who had killed himself with the cold premeditation shown by those letters, have done so without first removing the linen from his neck and otherwise preparing himself? When facing the scaffold the murderer dresses in his best, and however brutal and even brutish he may have been in life, he gives much and careful thought to looking decent after death. It seems absurd of course —this anxiety as to how one will look after death, more especially where, as in the case of the murderer, the body will be given up to the tender mercies of quick lime in an hour or two— and yet that this feeling does exist is admitted by every person. Does not one of your great English poets in 'The Ruling Passion

Strong in Death' put these words into the mouth of the dying coquette?

'One would not, sure, be frightful when one's dead
And, Betty, give this cheek a little red!'

"Now these men died in each instance without the slightest regard for the *convenances* of life or death, if I may be permitted to speak deprecatingly of the dead. They had not an atom of regard for after appearances, and glaringly belied human experience. But, unfortunate men, that was no fault of theirs. They were in fact surprised in the seclusion of their own rooms, where all busy and wearied men, thinking themselves secure from intrusion, avail themselves to the utmost of the few opportunities they have of being comfortably *en deshabille*.

"Moreover, they died without leaving behind them the faintest trace of any preparation beyond these formal letters announcing their intentions; such letters as, by the way, are rarely written by intending suicides.

"There is probably not one man amongst the millions on this globe who, if calmly contemplating suicide, would not leave behind him some evidence of preparation for the event; some last duty done, some last message of love or upbraiding to be delivered; yet I have been informed on good authority that there was, in every instance, an absolute omission of any such farewell message, as well as of all sign of preparation.

"On the contrary, there is considerable confusion in the business and also in the domestic affairs of the dead men, such as, from their well-known methodical habits, they would have been certain to provide against had they foreseen their end even thirty minutes.

"So looking to the utter absence in this case of that studied decorum in death observed by all men who do not slay themselves in the heat of passion, and also to the total lack of arrangement in the deceaseds' affairs, these facts alone would go far to prove that the dead men did not kill themselves, but, taking them in conjunction with the revealed forgeries, why, then, I say that the verdict of suicide is not to be maintained for a moment.

"But even that is not yet all"—and as my friend resumed he rose to his feet with a fire and force in his whole aspect which, together with his marvelous theory, affected me so powerfully that I, too, rose in sympathy, and we faced each other pale as death on the hearthrug. "No!" and the words came almost hissing from his lips, "these men were not *killed* by the wounds in their throats; they were killed—or at least the last one was killed—by the previous perforation of the base of the skull by a powerful needle or bodkin! I found a small bluish colored puncture at that point on the head of the last victim, and, on following it up by my directions, the surgeon discovered embedded in the brain, and penetrating half way through its entire depth, the needle-like blade of a small dagger.

"Stay!" protested my friend as I was about to speak, "that is not all! The blade had not been broken off; it had been released or discharged from its handle by a powerful spring at the moment of the stab with the intent that it should remain in the skull just beneath the surface and so stop all hemorrhage, and every trace of it be removed by the closing of the skin over it and by the natural covering of the hair.

"And even if the wound should bleed a little, the result would naturally be attributed to the greater wound in the throat.

"And now, my friend, can you conceive a more hideous plot, or one more fiendish in its ingenuity?"

When Pasquale had finished I felt benumbed with the force and fervor of his presentment of the case. To me he was no longer the gay, and brilliant friend, but the fierce and beautiful avenging angel of the murdered men, and repelled though I was by the horror which surrounded the series of crimes, I felt eager to aid him in his work of discovery.

"Have you taken any steps to find out whether the previous deaths were caused in the same way?"

As I put this question there was a knock at the door and Pasquale's austere valet handed his master a letter which had just arrived, and which being marked "immediate," he explained, he had taken the liberty of delivering at once.

In silence Pasquale handed me the letter, which stated briefly that in deference to his request an order had been obtained to exhume the bodies of the supposed suicides, with the result that in each case the same needle or dagger point had been found in the skulls of the deceased.

The writer, in conclusion, intimated that the bodies would be held until noon the following day in case Mr. Pasquale should wish to make any further inspection himself.

As I handed back the letter Pasquale dashed off a few lines by way of courteous acknowledgment, and stating that he would avail himself of the offer and call and examine the bodies the following day.

That night was one of the most agitated and unrestful in my hitherto placid life. For hours after Pasquale left I paced the floor of my room possessed with a fever of unrest and a frenzy of excitement which tore through my soul as a cyclone sweeps unresistingly through a bed of reeds. By the morning every thought and aspiration of my life lay prostrate before the one consuming desire to bring the murderer to justice.

At nine o'clock I arrived at my office pale and haggard, and a few minutes later I left to accompany my friend, excused from duty on the plea of urgent business.

When Pasquale and I entered the Mortuary Chamber, where the bodies awaited us, I shuddered for a moment and drew back. I had never seen a dead body and my whole soul shrank from the sight of a murderer's victims, in the various stages of decay. But after a time my courage returned; or it were, perhaps, more correct to say, a new impulse possessed me, and I went through the ordeal of the morning without further display of weakness.

There was little additional evidence gleaned; but when the four dagger points, which had been the means used to kill the murdered men, lay side by side on the table, they were found to be exact in size and shape, thereby proving beyond all doubt that the same hand had wrought all the murders.

My friend, who was examining the weapons carefully under the microscope, murmured to himself, "Antonio Seratzzi, Venice," and in response to the inquiry of my eyes he replied, "As nearly as I can decipher it for the rust, that is the name of the maker of these daggers. It seems to me that I have heard of them before, though for my life I can't recollect where or in what connection," and he put his hand to his forehead as if he were trying to recollect.

CHAPTER IV.

THE publication of the discovery that the supposed suicides were, in reality, murders committed by the same individual, filled London with horror, which was intensified a hundred-fold by the knowledge that the murderer was still at large.

The Metropolitan police, even when put upon the right track, failed to discover any clue of the murderer, and at the end of a fortnight all they could say in the way of elucidation was, that an aged man with long white hair had been seen near the scene of each of the murders at the time of the occurrence and prior to it.

There was nothing especially suspicious in his actions or appearance, and the fact that he was in the neighborhood at the time might simply be a coincidence, or the various testimony might not even refer to the same individual, for white-haired elderly men are not at all uncommon in London.

That the police should attach any importance to so faint a clue was perhaps the best evidence of their admission how completely they were baffled; so at least the public considered and the newspapers jeered the officials for their inefficiency.

Meantime my friend continued his investigation with unabated ardor, and, night after night, in the quiet of my bachelor rooms, we discussed each point of evidence, however slight, and classified or dismissed it according to its value.

Pasquale surrendered everything to the discovery of the dreadful mystery, and he grew thin and anxious-looking as the days passed by without throwing any further light upon it.

These were days ill-suited to hilarity, and much of the gaiety of Pasquale's sunny ways faded before their chilling influences; still if the efflorescence of his light-hearted disposition seemed shed for the time, the fact only served to reveal the true beauty of soul which was the foundation of all I loved so much.

Save when crossed by the sight of suffering uselessly inflicted upon the lower animals, I think he was the sweetest, gentlest creature God ever made; and the most lovable.

"And yet so inexorable in hunting down the assassin!" the reader will say—and I answer yes. Of the secret of that involved mechanism which formed Pasquale's soul I had no key; I only know that to me my friend was like the fascinating page of some dearly-loved book—blurred and unintelligible here and maybe there, but still sweeter in its occasional illegibility than all the other volumes on earth combined.

At the end of the third week of search Pasquale's valet called to explain that his master had suddenly been summoned abroad to a family council, but that his absence would probably not extend beyond a week.

If I could ever have found it in my heart to be vexed with Pasquale it would have been over his habit of obeying those calls so promptly as not even to allow himself time to bid me good-bye.

"Did your master leave no message, Jacques?" I inquired, puzzled to account for the absence of any further explanation.

"No, sir; he left in haste and ordered me to present his apologies to you for his omission to call and say good-bye."

I looked at the speaker and endeavored to read his expression, but the deep-set eyes dropped the moment they encountered my gaze, and the clear-cut cruel lips and formidable jaw, together with the down-cast eyes made one of the most unpleasing masks it had ever been my evil fortune to gaze upon.

I thought of the masks of murderers in Madame Tussaud's Chamber of Horrors, and began to regard my visitor with a curious interest.

"Will you have a glass of brandy, Jacques?" I inquired, piqued by the man's impenetrability, and trusting to the liquor to thaw it.

"Thank you, sir."

But the potent liquor served only to harden the deep lines which guarded the reticent lips, and after I had measured the implacable face and found no encouragement there, I said, "Jacques, that is all," and, with a low bow the inscrutable valet, or detective, left.

After he had closed the door, I amused myself by sketching his head in profile upon the blotting pad. As the sketch lay before me it certainly did not represent, according to either phrenologists or physiognomists, a bad or wicked head. It was simply the side face of a self-contained, determined man, and one possessed of considerable possibility of lofty purpose.

I tossed the paper from me—disappointed in the sketch even more than I had been in the original.

On the fourth day after my friend had left, I was aroused at an early hour by the valet, who, after apologizing for the intrusion, handed me the morning paper, and pointed to the announcement of another suicide by a public functionary, and under circumstances precisely similar to the cases which had preceded it.

As in the other instances, the victim's hand grasped a razor, to account for the deep wound in his throat, while his death was in reality due to the puncture of the brain by the concealed dagger point.

My instant impulse was to telegraph for my friend to enable him to take up the scent while it was fresh. I accordingly framed a message for the valet to send in his own name, and this I—still in bed—requested him to dispatch.

At four in the afternoon I received a note from the valet to the effect that he had heard from his master, and that the latter would be with me the following morning.

"Let me see the cablegram you received, Jacques." "Sorry that I have destroyed it," replied that irritating individual. I thought that in a gentle and careless way I would hint to my friend that however faithful a valet or detective Jacques might be, something less like a cast-iron sphinx would better meet the exigencies of ordinary life. I was undergoing a childish fit of annoyance.

The evening papers gave full details of the so-called suicide and also announced the fact that a white-bearded individual—such as the police had connected with the previous crimes—had been seen in the vicinity of the suicide, and had been traced.

Such was the condition of affairs when my friend, covered with the dust of travel, entered my room the following morning.

At his urgent and indeed impassioned request, I obtained leave of absence from the office that day, in order to aid him in following the clues left by the murderer while they were still fresh.

As I left my apartments with my friend, I caught sight of his valet standing at the entrance to the adjoining house. His usually stolid face seemed to be expressive of anxiety, and once or twice he moved as if about to speak. He had, however, all his life long cultivated a habit of silence, and in his present spasm of uncertainty it prevailed. I saw or appeared to see, a struggle going on in his mind, but I had no clue to his apprehensions, and the symptoms of his distress were too indefinite and too fleeting to justify action on my part; and, unwarned, unchecked by the hand which still, even at the eleventh hour, might have changed it, my friend Pasquale and I went forward to fulfil our destinies.

I would fain draw a curtain over the events of the following twenty-four hours. They have darkened my life, and they will shorten my days. Pasquale and I examined each detail of the murder, but without throwing further light upon it. The police, on their part, followed up step by step the retreat of the white-haired murderer, only, however, to lose him at King's Cross. He had been too astute to hail a cab, and the numerous exits afforded by that teeming centre gave him all the facilities for escape which he needed.

When we parted for the night it was in disheartened silence. True, Pasquale looked bright and cheery as usual, but I knew by my own feelings that he must be as low in spirits as could well be. In vain I strove to bury myself in an agreeable book; I could not read and I could not rest.

At length, worn out by the day's fierce though fruitless emotions, I threw myself, tired and worn out, on my bed, and after a while I fell into a deep and dreamless sleep.

Presently I awoke—suddenly and keenly conscious of the near happening of some event of stupendous importance. The fire in the grate was still burning brightly, so that I had not slept long. Why had I awoke so soon and in such a startled and expectant state?

There was no apparent reason within my room—but, hark! what was that? Clearly and distinctly, as if there were no obstructing walls, I could hear the noise made by the tenant of the neighboring rooms as he prepared himself to retire for the night. The sound of each movement fell on my ear, in my then state of tension, with all the clearness of a bell. I could even hear his muttered conversation. The latter seemed to be of so strange and disjointed a character that, my curiosity overcoming me, I stooped and applied my ear to the keyhole of the oaken door which divided our rooms, believing that some demented person had gained wrongful access to the adjoining rooms.

My view was limited to a few seconds, at the end of which the other door which fronted the one in my own wall was abruptly closed. But in that limited time my eye had garnered a terrible harvest, for in the muttering inmate of the adjoining room I had identified—or imagined I had identified—the white-bearded murderer as described by all who had seen him; not indeed identified to me by the whiteness of his hair and his age only, but by the blood-stained hands which he removed from his gloves and by the weapon which he laid upon his table.

What to do I knew not, and, horrified beyond measure, I

lay in my bed, petrified with apprehension, waiting for the dawn.

With the first glimmer of dawn I sent next door for my friend, and explained to him my midnight experiences.

"It is very strange," he murmured. "Very strange. Who do you think lives opposite to you?" From the glance he gave me it was evident that my friend thought I had taken leave of my senses. "Only the old Frenchman you told me of," I replied. "Old Frenchman?" he returned with an air of puzzled surprise and interrogation. "Did I say an old Frenchman lived over against you? You misunderstood me, I think; he occupies the rooms to the rear." "Well, it was there that I heard the noise and saw the man," I replied.

A look of pain and perplexity had come into my friend's face, and for a few minutes he sat in silence, apparently lost in thought. Then he rose to his feet and turned towards the door, adding as he opened it, "As soon as you have breakfasted I would like you to accompany me to the police station. I think you ought to tell the officers what you saw."

There was still the same look of puzzled uncertainty in my friend's face, as well as an anxious glance, as if for my welfare, but there was also a look of unutterable resolution as he said, as if to himself, "There must be no hesitation; this thing has to be gone through."

An hour later Pasquale and I arrived at the police station, and half an hour afterwards two police officers, two detectives, Pasquale and myself left for my friend's house.

On the way thither Pasquale stepped aside to make a small purchase. "Go straight on; I will follow you in a minute. I have left my pass-key in another pocket, so you must knock for admittance."

"Show these gentlemen up to the third floor." Such was the landlady's orders to the servant when we requested to be shown to Mr. Pasquale's rooms, where we were to mature our plans.

When the servant reached the second floor she threw open the front sitting-room door and stood aside to allow us to enter.

"This is not the third floor, my good girl," exclaimed the senior constable; "this is the second floor."

"Well, sir! mistress calls it the third floor," the servant replied.

At this moment Pasquale, who had joined us, remarked pleasantly, "The girl is right; her mistress is an American and counts the ground-floor as the first floor; these are the rooms which I occupy."

"Yes, sir," exclaimed the reassured servant, "these are Mr. Pasquale's rooms."

My brain was in a perfect whirl—these my friend's rooms! I had always imagined that he lived on the floor above, misled by the American landlady's method of reckoning the floors. I glanced at Pasquale, but he was unconscious of my look.

Turning to the servant he said, "Tell your mistress that the police wish to inspect M. Goddecourt's rooms, and bring us the key of his door."

"M. Leon Goddecourt is the elderly French gentleman I spoke to you about as occupying the rooms at the rear." This was Pasquale's explanation to me.

When the servant returned with the key Pasquale led the way into the passage communicating with the rooms at the back.

The occupant of the rooms was absent, and there was no hindrance to an exhaustive examination. There was no door connecting with the rooms of the house in which I lived. Nothing was discovered. The police were turning to go, impressed, I believe, with the idea that I had been hoaxing them, or else that the excitement of the murder had driven me crazy for the time, when Pasquale, addressing me, inquired whether I was certain that these were the rooms into which I was looking when I saw the supposed murderer. "You can see for yourself,

Wyndham," he remarked, "that your rooms and mine are not of the same length, and it was very easy for you to make a mistake by concluding that the dimensions were the same."

"I cannot tell with any certainty," I added falteringly, "for without thinking very closely about it, I had assumed that the rooms on both sides the partition were the same depth, but the door on my side is at the extremity of my bedroom, and when you said that the Frenchman lived at the rear, I concluded from the appearance of the man I saw that I was looking into his rooms."

"Well the matter can be settled very promptly," remarked Pasquale. "If you will go with one of these gentlemen, Wyndham, and show him the doorway through which you saw the old man, we can easily connect with you here."

This seemed the most natural thing to do, and we prepared to carry out Pasquale's suggestion. As I was leaving the room the police sergeant inquired whether Pasquale had the key of the door connecting my rooms with his through the wall dividing the two houses, and before I passed out of hearing I heard Pasquale explain that he had never had a key of that door, and did not believe that there was one in existence.

When the policeman and I entered my apartments the former remarked that he thought that the door which I pointed out to him would, if opened, be found to lead into Mr. Pasquale's rooms—"at least I judge so from the relative length of the rooms," he added.

Our loud knockings at the door through which I had seen the midnight spectacle produced no result for a minute; evidently our friends were still in the rear rooms. Then we could hear voices indistinctly, and presently the sound of blows opposite to us showed that our friends had at last "located" us.

After a short interval of heavy blows on the opposite door the latter was burst open—that much we could hear by the volume of sound which reached us—there was a shout of excitement, and presently the door which had been forced was shut, and we could see and hear no more.

Something very amazing had happened; what was it?

How can I relate the story of the events which followed? Even now, at this lapse of time, the recital of them chills my inmost soul. When we returned to the other house, we found Pasquale, my friend and more than brother, in the custody of the police. The space between the double doors dividing his room and mine had revealed all the paraphernalia of the supposed murderer, and that it belonged to Pasquale was apparently beyond doubt.

The wig and beard; the clothes, the boots, the blood-stained gloves; and even the hare's-foot with which the face had been painted to the semblance of age, all belonged to him and all were there; and worse and still more damning evidence was found in an oblong ivory box of antique pattern. Within this lay a stiletto handle, the ivory of which was yellow with extreme age. The weapon had no blade, but imbedded in the faded velvet of the lid were seven dagger points identical in every respect with those found in the heads of the dead men.

As we came forward the police sergeant removed a handkerchief from the pocket of the coat found in the recess.

It, too, was slightly stained with blood, and on the corner it bore the embroidered monogram of my ill-fated friend.

Horror-stricken, I stared at the face of Pasquale, who was now securely held by the police. Still the same puzzled expression in it; that and nothing more. He was evidently unable to understand the situation. After a time he heaved a deep sigh, and, stretching out his manacled hands, he took up the ivory dagger, as if casually and disinterestedly.

"Yes, that must have been what he used," he murmured; "I have read of such stilettos."

At that moment I caught the gaze of the valet, Jacques,

who had silently stolen into the room. I had, up to this time, well-nigh hated his homely, reticent face for the way it resisted me, but now and henceforward I loved it for the expression it bore on that fateful morning.

It was the appeal of a hero prepared to sacrifice his life on the mere fraction of a chance, and what his glance entreated was that I should create a diversion so that he should carry out his intentions. The hard lines on his inflexible face seemed to shiver and break in his terrible anxiety, and his fears, although they added to my own dread, inspired me.

"Stay!" I said to the officer, "I have a confession to make. This gentleman," pointing to Pasquale, "has done nothing; a child could see by his face that he is innocent. I am the guilty person; my room also opens on to that cupboard; I placed all the material of my make-up there, and raised the alarm to disguise my own guilt," and I held out my wrists as if to feel the clasp of the handcuffs.

At the conclusion of my remarks Jacques sprang forward like a tiger, hurled one detective to the floor, thrust the policemen swiftly on one side, and, seizing his master by the arm, was hurrying him away when a violent blow from the powerful and cool-headed sergeant disabled him.

"Arrest him," the sergeant said briefly, to his subordinates, indicating poor Jacques; then turning to myself, he pointed with his hand to the door opening into my room, of which the bolts were still shot in their sockets.

"I admire your efforts, sir, but you could not have entered that space between the two doors from your room, for it was bolted against you!"

Meantime, Pasquale appeared unconscious of the turmoil. He seemed still to be examining the stilettos.

Only once did he look up—when he heard me endeavoring to incriminate myself—then a soft beautiful smile crept over his face, but he nevertheless shook his head with inflexible determination.

"You must accompany me, sir," said the sergeant to Pasquale.

"To jail?" inquired the other. "A Pasquale to jail!" and he laughed softly, as if the thought amused him.

"Good-bye, Wyndham, dear old friend, faithful to the last; Heaven send you the best of luck," and he kissed me fondly and even passionately on both cheeks. "God bless you twice over, once for yourself and once for me, who never had a blessing;" and as he spoke a tremor shook his frame and he was barely able to steady himself.

"And, Jacques, my faithful friend and guardian, God bless you too—pray for me."

Then his gaze grew dim with tears and he turned again to the strange weapon still lying on the table.

"Who would have thought that these little bodkins could have wrought such fearful havoc?" As he spoke he took up one of the steel points and fitted it mechanically into its socket.

It was all over in a moment. With a rapid movement Pasquale directed the point towards himself, his wrist turned slightly, the hand tightened fiercely and then opened, and the ivory handle of the stiletto rolled on the floor as Pasquale reeled and fell into the arms of those behind him. His eyes opened wide, smiled the old smile into mine just for one brief instant, then the darkness of death blotted out their light, and the lids drooped slowly as if from overwhelming fatigue. Pasquale had entered into the rest which knows no waking.

They thought that he had fainted, but I knew differently. The deadly stiletto had done its last work faithfully and fatally. The quick turn of the wrist and the fierce grasp of the weapon had released the powerful spring concealed in the ivory handle, and the dagger point was now imbedded in Pasquale's heart.

A week later two visitors entered my rooms. They were

my dead friend's father and the valet, Jacques. From the former I learned that his son had, for some years, been subject to fits of dementia. These usually occurred during the full moon. Mr. Pasquale's reason for sending his son to London was a hope expressed by the family doctor that an entire change of scene might strengthen his mind and his body, and be the means of creating a break in those periodic attacks.

Jacques, the valet, was in reality a faithful servant of the family, employed from the first to take care of his young master. He had occupied the adjoining room with Pasquale from the date of his first arrival, but he kept himself very much in the background, as Pasquale was extremely sensitive lest his condition should become known; a fact which explained his, to me, unaccountable objection to receiving me in his rooms.

After the return from Paris, Jacques, as the reader is aware, took a more prominent part in his master's daily life, for it was then that I saw him for the first time. This greater prominence was due to the fact that Jacques had reported to Mr. Amidio Pasquale, senior, that the attacks instead of becoming more feeble, were growing more marked month by month.

Jacques explained that the sudden alleged departure of his young master was due to the fact, that, feeling the approach of the mental disorder, he would without delay place himself in his valet's hands. He was in nowise a prisoner, for from the first to the last there had not been, on the part either of his family or of his so-called valet, the faintest suspicion of a homicidal mania; the only objects of the secrecy being a general watchfulness in case of fresh developments, and to keep his infirmity from the knowledge of his friends.

There were days when Pasquale felt out of sorts and indisposed, and since it was the orders of his medical man that he should be soothed and not opposed at such periods, the valet made no intrusion on his privacy then.

It was undoubtedly at such periods that my friend's most

serious attacks had culminated in the atrocities already recorded, for of his connection with these, subsequent investigations removed every shadow of doubt.

As for the apparent difficulty in crossing the Channel to England, and committing a murder, without his absence being discovered by his friends that was readily explained. He had never while in Paris been under strict surveillance, and he was frequently absent for a few days at a time at a friend's house.

It was evident that plans conceived during one period of lunacy were perfected during the next, or following periods. This was especially evident in connection with the dead man's efforts to obtain specimens of the hand-writing of the men whom he had resolved to kill, and had afterwards killed.

In the closet where the disguise was found—in which I had seen my friend arrayed, in that awful midnight glance,—were discovered letters from six well-known justices of the peace, five of whom, including the chief of the police, had undoubtedly died by Pasquale's hand. These letters were evidently in reply to cunningly worded inquiries, such as would be likely to induce the recipients to answer with their own hands. This had been done in every case but one (the sixth letter had been dictated); and the lengthy epistles which the unsuspecting justices had written afforded Pasquale, then in the fulness of his madness, ample opportunity of making himself acquainted with their handwritings, and so enabled him to forge the farewell letters by each supposed suicide, without fear of detection.

If further proof of my demented friend's guilt had been wanted, it was readily forthcoming in the drafts of the letters to the justices found in his handwriting in the same recess.

The horrible feeling, akin to remorse, which I experienced on recognizing that it was my evidence as to the aged figure which I had seen at midnight in the adjoining room, that had resulted in my friend's arrest and suicide, was somewhat mitigated when I learned that on the morning of the discovery the superintendent of police at Scotland Yard had received by the first post a communication from the expert employed by my dead friend to examine the letters left by the supposed suicides, to the effect that having detected a certain resemblance in the handwriting in Pasquale's letter to that in the forgeries, he had made a crucial examination, with the result of satisfying himself that the two were identical.

On the strength of that evidence a warrant would have been obtained against Pasquale that day had not events rendered it unnecessary.

Nor was that all. On the superintendent's desk I saw the five letters which had elicited the replies found in the recess. These a keen detective had discovered among the papers of the dead man, when in search of some trace as to the methods employed to obtain specimens of their handwriting. These letters requested a reply to Amidio Pasquale, P. O. Box No. 2034, presumably to avoid their delivery at the house at unseasonable times, and indicating that Pasquale, mad, was on his guard against Pasquale, sane. So that on all sides the net had been closing in around my dear demented friend.

Why, then, did Fate so gratuitously add to my lot the painful reflection that I had, by my ill-timed discovery, precipitated my friend's death? These additional links proved how boundless the resources of Destiny are when her time has arrived; surely, then, she might have spared me that last bitter drop which she had added to my brimming cup.

My task is done. With Pasquale's tragic ending a shadow settled upon me, and it has never wholly lifted. Our friendship lives in my memory as the one green and sunny oasis in my desert life, and here, far away from the home of my youth, I sit and muse on the gladsome hours we spent together—my only grounds for belief that there is a happier world beyond.

The man I knew—the friend I loved so passionately, the gentle-hearted creature to whom the pain of any creature which God had made was torture—was unconscious of the acts and ignorant of the identity of Pasquale the insane murderer. That much, wise physicians, versed in the mysteries of the human brain, have told me; and that I at least never for an instant doubted.

It may be that Pasquale's disorder was mentally contagious, and that my open and receptive mind imbibed some of the fatal theories which at times overbalanced his brilliant intellect. I almost hope that it is so, for it will extenuate the wicked rebellious thoughts which still surge through my brain when I recall the steps, one by one, which led to the final ending.

The thought of the loving and gentle Pasquale, fierce only in the pursuit of wrong, bringing all the marvelous resources of his wonderful brain to the discovery of that terrible London mystery, and unraveling it thread by thread only to weave it anew into a noose for himself, paralyzes my brain. Did ever human being before lead justice step by step through such a labyrinth of crime, and so unweariedly, until he brought her to the very threshold of murder, and face to face with himself the unconscious murderer!

I left my rooms hastily, and in disorder, as if invaded by the plague. Once only I unintentionally passed the house, and through the doorway of my cab I saw the dull, dusty windows of an empty residence, with the legend "To be let" placarded on the ill-fated No. 13.

THE
LOST WEDDING-RING.

CHAPTER I.

"Do you think it unlucky, then, to take off one's wedding-ring?"

The inquiry sprang with a half-startled air of surprise and alarm from a pair of pretty half-parted lips, and still more eagerly from two heavily-fringed and expressive gray eyes.

"Yes, dear, very unlucky; you ought to leave it where your husband placed it; it is like undoing the ceremony to take it off."

This most depressing reply was made with an air of conviction which greatly disturbed the fair questioner—the bride of a month—who had in a childish fit of restlessness removed her wedding-ring and was engaged testing the stupendousness of its avoirdupois on the coral tips of her dainty fingers.

Slowly, and as if it were something uncanny, the truant hoop was slipped back to its place, as the delicate flush on the young wife's cheek deepened with the dawning consciousness of a hitherto unknown crime.

"I wish you would tell me why you think so, grandma," was the somewhat timid rejoinder.

The elder lady's busy hands had dropped on her knees, and her face wore the absent-minded expression which told that "her eyes were with her heart, and that was far away."

The question was evidently unheard, and it was presently amended.

"Grandma, dear, has your wedding-ring never been off your finger since grandpa placed it there?"

The second question recalled the old lady's wandering thoughts, and she replied with a falter in her voice which heightened the look of alarm on her grand-daughter's face.

"Yes, dear, once."

"Oh! did anything happen?"

"Yes, love, something which I will never forget as long as I live."

As the elder lady spoke, the color faded slowly from the cheeks of the youthful bride, leaving the glowing eyes doubly dark by contrast with their pallor.

"Don't you think that it is growing cold, grandma?"

This was said with a little shiver, and looking up, the latter recognized for the first time that her remarks had startled and alarmed her grand-daughter.

"Mind you, Alice," she added hastily, "I do not mean to say that misfortune *always* follows, for of course a very great many people take off their wedding-rings sooner or later, apparently without any serious consequences, and I don't think that anything really threatens the happiness of a married couple unless the ring is actually lost; still, my dear — — "

The sound of a rapid, manly tread advancing on the arbor where the two were seated caused the bride to spring to her feet with a glad cry.

For a moment the husband caught a glimpse of a pair of swimming gray eyes with a world of woe reflected in their shadowy depths; the next a trembling pliant figure was nestling in his arms, and trying to explain amid tearful sobs about the bad luck coming to them both through the removal of the wedding-ring.

As soon as the astonished husband could frame an intelligible meaning out of the story, told with many interruptions of sobs and kisses and passionate hugs, he burst into a merry laugh.

"Why, you little silly!" he began, but his voice melted to a tenderness inarticulate in words, although mutually intelligible in love's rich vocabulary.

"Dear, *dear, dear!* to think what a sweet little goose it is after all," commenced the husband, after love's exactions had been religiously complied with. "Why, I know ladies who are continually losing their wedding-rings. There is Mrs. North for instance — — "

"O, George!!"

"Well," resumed the husband a little confusedly, "I know, of course, that she and her husband do not get on very well together, but there are others. There is—let me see—but never mind—I'll tell you what I'll do. I will take the ring off your finger myself and put it on again, *then* that will make everything just as it was," and with this pleasing little sophistry both bride and groom were made happy once more.

As the youthful pair left the arbor, the old lady, whose loving heart was wont to grow young again as she contemplated the happiness of the others, softly rubbed the mists from her glasses as she said with a sigh, "O, I wish Alice had not taken off her wedding-ring!"

CHAPTER II.

THAT the shadows of anxiety had not been altogether dispelled from the breast of the young bride, Alice Montgomery, was rendered apparent to her grandmamma the following morning, when the exactions of business had emptied the house of its male population.

The two ladies were seated on a broad piazza, whose columns and roof were richly festooned with a wealth of luxuriant creeper which the gentle breeze, creeping up from the meadows and laden with the smell of the hay-field, just stirred and no more.

For awhile the two sat in silence, their busy fingers and the placid movement of their rocking-chairs keeping up a kind of rhythmical flow of action as soothing as the "creen" of the tidal ebb and flow on a pebbly shore.

"Grandma," said Alice somewhat suddenly, letting her work fall on her lap, "I can't get out of my head what you said about the ill-luck in removing one's wedding-ring. George says that it is all an old superstition, and one quite exploded now; but when he leaves me to myself I get quite frightened about it—so, if you don't mind, dear, I wish you would tell me just what happened after you took off your ring."

"Alice, dearest, I wish you would forget all about it; your husband is quite right, it is just an old superstition."

But Alice was not to be turned from her inquiry, and with gentle feminine persistency she shook her pretty head, implying that life would be a burden to her until this terrible affair was cleared up.

"*Please*, grannie," was the extent of her audible entreaty, but her eyes contained a fervor of appeal which was entirely irresistible, and the old lady, who had by long experience learned the wisdom of an early capitulation to the "little gray eyes," as she called her grandchild, surrendered with a sigh of protest.

As she removed her spectacles from her face she became

aware of a strangely intent look suddenly visible on the face of her grand-daughter, who was looking at a clump of trees in the distance.

"What do you see, dear?" she inquired.

"I saw a figure in the copse yonder, which I fancied I recognized, but I must have been mistaken, and the person, whoever he was, has gone away?"

"Was he looking this way?"

"Yes, grandma, and I imagined for a moment that he was beckoning to me, but of course that could not be."

"Do you know, darling," exclaimed the elder lady in a tone of concern, "you must really not be so nervous; you will be fancying all kinds of things if you give way to such hallucinations. I am afraid that trouble of your brother's has affected your health. George must take you for a change of air."

The heightened color on the face of the youthful bride, which had aroused the other's anxiety, slowly faded from her face, leaving it pale and wan.

By way of reply, Alice stole to her grandmother's side, and brushing away the silvery hair with which the rising breeze was playing, imprinted a loving kiss on the time-furrowed brow.

"Never mind my fads, dear, tell me your story," she whispered in the other's ear, but there was a wistfulness in the tone which impressed her aged relation painfully, and she murmured, as the other sank to her seat, "I wish you would not insist, Alice."

"O, indeed I do, grandma," promptly replied the other.

"When I married your grandpa, dear," began the old lady, I was in delicate health. My mother had only recently died, and the fever to which she had succumbed had wasted my strength also. What with the weakness resulting from my illness and grief at the death of my mother, who had been my only remaining relative, and to whom I was naturally passionately attached, my health was completely broken down, and it was only the urgent wishes of your grandpapa, to whom I had been engaged to be married for more than a year, that I consented to the ceremony at such a time. I felt that I must have change of air, and quickly too, to avoid a complete collapse, and alone in the world as I was, I could not bear to go away and leave behind me the only being that I loved and that loved me.

"Henry too, 'urged me sair,' as the old Scottish ballad says, and told me that he could readily make arrangements for a six months' leave of absence, so that we could spend the winter-months, which were approaching, in the South.

"After the wedding we sailed for Florida, which was at that time enduring one of its occasional, but short-lived, bursts of prosperity. In the old days, long before the war, the State was making money, and the Florida planter as a potentate ranked side by side with the wealthy slave-owner of Mississippi and Louisiana.

"A friend of my husband's family had a plantation on the Gulf coast of Florida, below Cedar Keys. We had received a pressing invitation to spend our honeymoon on that plantation, and there we finally arrived early in the month of December, after a most delightful voyage.

"At Cedar Keys we had changed our ocean-going ship for a smaller coasting vessel, and as we sailed in our new craft up the waters of the Homosassa River, I thought that not even in my dreams had I pictured, 'a world so fair.' The broad, swelling bosom of the river, the luminous transparency of the atmosphere, the banks covered with a wealth and majesty of tropical trees, and the numerous coral islands dotting the centre of the river and crowned with a perfect glory of foliage,—all these thrilled my soul with a sense almost of religious devotion, just as some rare anthem, pealing from some old-world organ, will move the soul to an ecstasy of religious feeling.

"The planter and his family gave us a hearty welcome when at length our vessel cast anchor off the plantation landing.

"Their house was a large, rambling, frame building, with the negro quarters situated at some distance in the rear, and hidden from view by a heavy belt of orange and banana trees.

"The land was what is termed hard-wood, hammock land, which is considered to possess the richest soil in Florida. The Seminole Indians, of which there were several thousand still left in the State, always lived in the hammocks, and the plantation had formerly been the home of the celebrated chief, Osceola, of whom you have read so much.

"Colonel Andrews, who owned the plantation, had always been on excellent terms with the Indians, and among his frequent visitors was Tallahassee, the hereditary Grand Mico of the Seminoles, the brave and handsome young warrior-chief of the tribe.

"Shortly after we arrived at the plantation, Tallahassee made one of his customary visits, bringing with him an old warrior of his tribe and three younger chiefs.

"Colonel Andrews had allowed the Seminoles to build a few wigwams in an old hammock near his house, and in these the Indians lived during their visits.

"Our host was a widower, with two sons, and his house was managed by the usual retinue of colored servants. There was no white woman about the place, and I was probably one of the first of that color which the celebrated chief had ever seen.

"Tallahassee, although grave and silent like the rest of his race, and dignified as became the supreme authority in a still powerful tribe, manifested considerable interest in our excursions, and as he knew every foot of the vast forests, and every landing-place on the great rivers which were close at hand, his unobtrusive presence was always very welcome.

"Gradually a warm friendship, though for the most part undemonstrative, so far as he was concerned, grew up between us, and my husband was wont to declare, with much quiet amusement, that I had made a great conquest, and that the renowned warrior-king, Tallahassee, was in love with me.

"Of course, that was only his silly nonsense, and the expressive glances of the Indian's dark eyes were only the result of a certain taciturnity of habit enforced by the danger of talking when it might be that concealed enemies were near. With the Indians the eyes are wont to conduct the necessary conversation more readily than the slower and more dangerous tongue.

"On one occasion the Indian chief, our host, my husband and myself, started in a boat to examine the marvelous source of the Homosassa River, a few miles distant.

"This wonderful river springs a full-fledged flood from the ground, and is already a hundred yards in width within that distance of its spring, and so deep as to be navigable to moderate-sized craft.

"When our boat entered the cove where the river took its origin, it was with a feeling of fearful awe that I experienced the sensation of floating between heaven and earth. Above us was the pure ether, walled in on three sides by giant palms; beneath us lay a stupendous well of water, clear as the atmosphere above us, and calm and silent as the grave.

"Far down in its transparent depths we could distinctly see every tint and every movement of the smallest fish, just as clearly, in fact, as we could see the movement and brilliant hues of the birds and insects flitting to and fro between the trees overhead.

"To me, unaccustomed to such wonders, the scene verged on the supernatural, and I felt as if there was something uncanny in it,—a feeling destined soon to be intensified a thousand-fold. In order to illustrate the transparency of the water, which was there some forty feet in depth to the peddled bottom, my husband threw some small silver coins, one after another, into the spring, in which, contrary to expectation, there were no air bubbles to distract the view. As we watched them falling down through the water, slowly, as a feather falls through the air, it seemed almost as if they would never reach the bottom. At last, one of these coins fell between two great rocks, directly under us, which the shadow of our boat had prevented us from seeing sooner.

" 'Let the Water-Lily look,' exclaimed the Indian, pointing to the coin falling, and calling me by the poetic name with which he was accustomed to designate me.

"As the small silver piece glanced between the dark rocks it seemed to illuminate the gray blackness in which their narrow walls plunged the space between them, until finally the shadow hid it while still falling from sight.

" 'Great Heavens!' I exclaimed shudderingly, 'how deep is the water between those rocks?'

" 'Ah! who knows,' replied my husband.

"For a while a spell of silence fell upon us as we lay in the welcome shadow of the fringed palms, so deliciously cool after the heat of the exposed river.

"All at once the accident you wish to hear about happened. In order to cool my fevered hands I had been trailing my fingers to and fro through the cold spring water of the well. The downward position of my fingers, and the shrinking of the flesh in the cold water, consummated the catastrophe, and as I straightened my fingers to point to a strange variety of fish, my wedding-ring—already somewhat large for my hand, emaciated by long sickness—slipped from my finger, and slid into the water beneath us.

"The scream which burst from my lips directed my companions to the accident, and throwing off his hat and shoes my husband plunged headlong after the fallen ring.

"The Indian had risen hastily to his feet in the attempt to prevent my husband, but before he could get past me in the frail boat it was too late.

"My husband was as visible to us as if he had been in the air above instead of the water underneath. I knew him to be a strong swimmer, so although his plunge had somewhat unnerved me, I did not feel alarmed for his safety.

"But *what* a time it took him to get to the bottom! It seemed as if, struggle as he might, he would never reach it. The fact is, the powerful though unseen current of the giant spring was pressing him upwards with an almost irresistible force.

"At last, grasping with one firm hand the point of a rock in order to enable him to retain his position, he stooped to seize the ring. But it had fallen between two pieces of broken coral, and for a while which seemed long to us, but which was probably five or six seconds, it evaded his grasp. At last his fingers closed upon it, and he was about to turn in order to ascend to the surface when a hoarse cry from the Indian caused us to follow the direction of his pointed hand.

"Oh! Alice, child, to this day it chills my soul to tell you what I saw there.

"Out from those ghostly, ill-fated rocks I told you of, a gigantic alligator had floated up like some horrible creature from the nether world, and I could see the lurid fire of its red eyes and the gleam of its wide open jaws, as, with a mighty swish of its great tail, it rushed at my husband, its great body shrouding him from view as with a gruesome mantle.

"I saw Tallahassee, knife in hand, and with his long, and hitherto pliant hair bristling like a mane, spring headlong from the boat, and I felt the frail craft rock beneath me from the shock, and then I think I must have become unconscious for a few seconds.

"When my senses returned and I opened my eyes, I saw Colonel Andrews staring, rifle in hand, and with horrified, helpless gaze, into the waters which were now red with blood and boiling with some awful invisible conflict. What, in God's great name, was going on in the now hidden depths? I felt as if my brain was giving way, and in my frenzy I strove to throw myself into the water to die with my dear husband if I could not save him. With gentle but firm hand Colonel Andrews restrained me.

" 'Hold that, and if you see anything *shoot*,' he exclaimed, giving me his rifle, 'I am going to help my friends.'

"But before he had finished speaking, the violent lashing of the waters ceased, and almost instantly the dark head of the Indian appeared above the crimsoned waters. 'Alone?' Ah no, God be praised, not alone. Across his shoulder lay the blood-stained and insensible body of my dear husband, whom he had snatched from the jaws of death, and worse than death; and, child, from that instant I have loved the whole Indian race.

"With a few vigorous strokes the Indian reached the shore where he gently deposited the insensible form of my husband. After a lapse of time, which seemed an eternity to me, the efforts of Tallahassee and Colonel Andrews were successful, and my poor husband began to breathe once more. With ready knife the Indian cut the shirt sleeve from his right arm and shoulder which were terribly torn and disfigured by the alligator's cruel teeth. The shoulder-blade was fractured and the arm broken by the bite.

"As my husband's eyes opened and rested on my woe-begone face, a faint, wan smile crept over his features. He was unable to articulate, but his eyes glanced expressively towards his right arm. I thought he was indicating his injury and showed my distress, but he gently shook his head and whispered faintly, 'My hand.'

"He could not move his wounded arm but I took his rigidly clenched hand in mine and gently strove to open it; but the fingers were set in their grasp, and I was afraid to use any force. A look of disappointment crept over his face, and he murmured weakly, 'Open it.'

"I did so; and oh, child, what do you think I saw? There, embedded in his palm, with the fury of his grasp when he found death setting in, was my poor wedding-ring, come back from the depths to me.

"My feelings overwhelmed me, and I well-nigh sobbed my life out on my husband's breast.

"The huge alligator had seized my husband by the arm, and in spite of his efforts had dragged him to the edge of the deep cleft. In another instant rescue would have been hopeless, but in that instant the Indian's knife had been driven up to the hilt in the eyes of the great saurian, with lightning-like rapidity. The blows blinded the alligator, and the pain caused him to loosen his hold. His frantic struggles were the result of the continued contest with the Indian. My husband became insensible from long submersion by the time he was released from the alligator."

When the elder lady finished her tragic story the younger one crept softly to her side, and the tears stole down her cheeks as she buried her face on the other's shoulder murmuring, "Oh poor, poor grannie, what a terrible ordeal it must have been to go through."

After the acute feelings naturally called up by the narration of so painful an incident had subsided, the young wife inquired why she had never been told of the terrible affair before.

"Because, dear, I have shuddered even to think of the thing, it left such a horrible impression on my mind."

"Dear grannie," murmured the other sympathetically. "Oh, if one tenth of the misery which you endured happens to me through the removal of *my* ring, I know I shall die, I could never stand any great strain; people were stronger then than they are now.

"I wonder, grannie, what you were like when you were my age," resumed the speaker; "have you no old miniatures among your collections of relics?"

"No, my dear, but I have an old scrap-book which contains a drawing of myself, sketched during my honeymoon by my husband, who was quite a famous etcher before that accident to his arm. There is also, I think, an etching of Tallahassee, and one of the old plantation."

Very naturally, nothing would content the youthful bride until she had seen the drawings, and her grandmamma left the piazza to fetch the album.

When left alone, an anxious expression crept over the former's face, and the point of her tiny boot tapped the boarded floor, nervously and somewhat impatiently.

"I wonder if that *was* Tom whom I saw beckoning to me in the thicket, and if so, what trouble has he been getting into now?"

At that moment a low voice called her softly by name, and suppressing the scream of alarm which rose to her lips, she turned to find the person of whom she was thinking, her scapegrace brother Tom, half hidden in the shrubbery which separated the main building from some outhouses.

Before she could frame any greeting, a letter fluttered to her feet, and the alarming visitor disappeared as her grandmamma returned, album in hand.

All that the letter said, when surreptitiously opened, was, "I *must* meet you at the end of the peach walk at eight to-night; don't fail to be there; my safety concerned."

Meantime, with spectacles adjusted, the old lady with gentle fingers turned over the leaves of the antiquated album, now yellowed with its half century of age.

"There, Alice," she at last exclaimed, "there is my likeness, and really, dear, it is as like you as it can be, or else my old eyes are deceiving me."

"Oh, grannie, it *is* a beauty—like me, is it? Ah! you are flattering me, and yet, really, truly, I almost seem to be gazing at myself when I look at it. I hope, dearest, I shall be as beautiful as you are when I am old; but I think only a good life can make a handsome old age."

By way of reply the other stroked the beautiful dark brown hair which frowned over the fair Grecian features, and murmured, "You will *always* be beautiful, my darling; God has given you not only a beautiful face, but a beautiful and unselfish disposition to match it."

"Oh, grandma! is that splendid-looking Indian Tallahassee?" inquired Alice, pointing to a well-executed etching of an Indian chief, evidently of the Seminole tribe, from the turbaned head and long-waving locks.

"Yes, dear, that is our noble friend, Tallahassee."

Long the young wife's eyes gazed on the spirited etching, which revealed an Indian warrior or buck in his youthful prime, his luminous eyes and handsome aquiline features dignified with all the Seminole pride of race, but wearing, as well, a certain refinement of expression rarely seen except in very highly civilized society.

But it is very doubtful if the young wife's attention was riveted on the Indian's likeness, for when she raised her head, there was an air of troubled perplexity visible on her face which the inspection of the portrait could not account for. Was she thinking of her ill-starred brother?

"What you must have suffered, *dear* grannie. I wonder you could ever bear to hear the name of Florida again."

"No, dear, I have none of that feeling. Some of the happiest moments of my life were spent there, and I am hopeful that I may visit it once again, now that it is so easy of access.

"I wonder whether our old friend, Tallahassee, has forgotten us yet."

"Why, surely he is not living yet!" exclaimed the granddaughter in an astonished voice.

"Yes, dear, I believe he is; he certainly was alive a year ago, although he is now an old and heartbroken man. The settlement of the State by emigrants has driven him from his old haunts and from every new home as fast as he has made it, and the tribe has dwindled down to a mere handful of followers and himself; the very tender mercies of the pale face are cruel to the red man."

"But did he own no land?"

"His tribe thought they owned it all, but the white man came and wrested it from them, and although our own Government always promised to give Tallahassee a Reservation of his own, it was never done, and now the old warrior has not even land of his own sufficient to be buried in."

"What a shame! Is it the fault of the Government?"

"I think it is the fault of the Indian Department. I don't think the officials had any bad intentions towards Tallahassee and his Seminoles, who have always been entirely friendly to the whites, but there was no one to urge the red man's claim, and so the thing drifted from session to session while matters grew worse for the Indians every year. Ah! it is very true that 'evil is wrought by want of thought as well as want of heart.' "

"I wish George was a Senator; I would get him to press poor dear old Tallahassee's claim," murmured the young wife in half soliloquy, for which tender-hearted little speech the old lady kissed her affectionately as they passed indoors together.

CHAPTER III.

NOTWITHSTANDING the day's outward sense of joyousness and rest, in the brilliant sun, softened breeze, and lovely landscape, there was trouble brewing for the peaceful New England home, and one, at least, of its inmates seemed conscious of the fact.

"I wonder," exclaimed Alice, as she stood before the cheval glass in her dressing-room, attending to those delicate personal adornments with which youthful brides are wont to prepare to receive their lords and masters, "I wonder whether grandma would have told me that terrible story about her wedding-ring if she had known that I had really lost mine?"

This momentous question was asked of her *vis-à-vis*, her own brilliant reflection in the swinging mirror before her. As the young bride turned with a look of inquiry to her image in the glass, we may be permitted a passing glance at the reflection which met her gaze.

A tall and lissom figure, with all the graceful lines of the stately Grecian form, combined with the warmer and more womanly outlines of the Norman maiden, the youthful matron stood a vision of loveliness which Praxiteles himself might have despaired to reproduce.

As she tossed the burden of brown tresses from her forehead, her pure Grecian profile stood out clear and delicate as a cameo against the curtain of dark hair which fell, a rippling sombre cascade, almost to her feet. The dark eyes smiled back a sympathetic glance from the mirror, and then a weary sigh of anxiety clouded the beautiful eyes with trouble. Why?

The conversation about the removed ring had been resumed in the morning, and in compliance with the husband's request, the young bride had again taken off her wedding-ring, in order that he might himself replace it on her fair finger; this unfortunately happened on the upper piazza, and in the usual loving conflict with which youthful couples adjust all matters between themselves, the ring had fallen into the garden and mysteriously disappeared.

Search had been made high and low, but unavailingly, and with a feeling of alarm which each concealed from the other, but which, nevertheless, almost bordered on despair, the subject was dropped with mutual consent.

"It is just as well," said the husband, with simulated cheerfulness; "I will bring you a fresh ring to-night, and I will put that on your finger myself—*once for all.*"

"Ah, pet, but it won't be *our* ring," the bride had exclaimed with a tremor in her voice, and although the husband had ridiculed the idea that it made any difference, he was painfully conscious of the look of gentle reproach in the outraged eyes of his young wife and of the justice of it.

Punctually at five o'clock the coachman brought around the carriage in which his young mistress was accustomed to drive to the station to meet her husband. The train arrived punctually, but it brought no husband to the waiting wife. It was her first disappointment, trivial in character though it might be, and to the youthful bride it was painful almost beyond expression. As the coachman drove home it required a brave effort to still the quivering lip and to press back the too ready tear.

"Oh, I hope," she murmured fearfully, "that this is not the beginning of any trouble through the loss of my wedding-ring." For a moment the thought appalled her, and then a smile of wonderful relief flashed across her face.

"Oh! how silly I am," she exclaimed, chiding herself, "of course George is late because he has to buy me a new ring."

This explanation was entirely sufficient, and the once more radiant bride ascended to her room humming a dainty little operatic air, as happy as the mocking-bird which flooded the sunny stairway with melody.

But the shadow returned to the young wife's face with

ever-deepening gloom when the six o'clock and seven o'clock trains arrived and brought no husband with them.

"He is detained on business, dear," explained her grandma.

"Why couldn't he telegraph then?"

"There is no office within five miles, love, and no doubt he thought he would get here before his message."

But another trouble weighed—and heavily—upon the young bride's mind. The last train was due at eight o'clock, the hour so urgently appointed by her brother for their interview. How *could* she possibly meet both her husband and her brother at the same time?

This brother was a sad scapegrace, and it had been the one mistake of the bride's married life not to mention his existence to her husband.

"Why don't you tell your husband about Tom?" had urged the old lady.

"O, I can't bear George to know that I have anybody disgraceful so nearly related to me; if ever he misunderstood any of my actions, or if I was not at hand to explain them, he would be certain to think that I was going wrong, like poor Tom, and it would break my heart. Don't you remember, dear, that night when we were talking about the Wollanders, how scornfully he said: 'Oh, they couldn't run straight to save their lives—it is in the blood—the strain is bad.' That sentence of George's determined me not to tell him anything."

"Believe me, dearest," replied the other, "it was a mistake, and one which grows more serious the longer it is kept up."

"O, I *could not* tell him," returned Alice with a little air of determination; "but, grannie, dear, don't-ee scare me like that."

And so the matter had ended for that time, and fair Alice's opportunity was lost forevermore.

When Mr. Montgomery arrived by the eight o'clock train

and found no one to meet him, a dull feeling of apprehension crept into his heart. His first thought was, "Can my darling be sick? She is in very delicate health."

With hasty steps he sped on his homeward way, denouncing the special business which on that particular day had detained him.

"I'm glad I thought to buy the ring during the day and did not leave it till after business, or I should either have lost the last train or had to come home without the ring."

Entering the house unseen, by the side door, he glanced through the empty reception rooms, noted the vacant dining-room, and then hastened upstairs to his wife's apartments, only, however, to find these silent and deserted.

A feeling of uneasiness and oppression took possession of him. "Where can everybody be?" he muttered. "Ah! there are grandpa and grandma coming across the fields, but where is Alice?"

Hastily glancing across the grounds from the window of his wife's boudoir, he caught a glimpse in the gathering dusk of feminine apparel at the end of the long peach walk. The light was too uncertain, the distance too great, and the foliage too thick for accurate observation, but it appeared to him that some member of the household, probably one of the maids, was keeping a somewhat late appointment out of doors, for, with the aid of a pair of opera-glasses taken from the adjoining table, he could discern the dark outline of a man's dress in close proximity to the other and more flowing garment.

Presently the two figures parted, and in the person of the female now hurrying down the peach walk toward the house, the astonished husband recognized his wife.

For a moment he stood gazing, stolidly it seemed, out of the window. Only the dull leaden look creeping over his face, and, presently, the panting breath gave indication of the shock he had received.

That his wife, whom he had considered as pure as the angels in Heaven, should take advantage of his first absence to meet another man clandestinely—another man! Bah! an old lover, for did she not kiss him at parting? Yes, that much the glasses had enabled him to see. The thought was agony, a thousand times worse than death.

"Oh, Alice! Alice! my love, my wife! How *could* you!" he cried to the unhearing walls, as he put his hand to his head with a gesture of infinite pain.

That, however, was the last wail of love's weakness; then the frenzy of jealousy and revenge seized him and possessed him like a demon, and the look on his face, as he took a revolver from a secret panel in the bureau, boded ill for his future happiness.

"Fooled, the very first month of my marriage too!" he muttered; and the words seemed ground out between his clenched teeth.

"——But I will clear this thing up or put an end to it once for all, even if in doing so I have to put an end——"

His voice sank as he passed from a side door and stole rapidly through the garden to intercept the man who had just left his wife.

The narrow path through the woods brought him out, as he had anticipated, in advance of the person whom he had come to meet.

He saw him coming along a hundred yards or so away, and he felt, mixed up with his murderous feelings, a craving to see the face of the man for whom his wife had forgotten him even in their honeymoon.

The stranger bade him good-evening with an easy, nonchalant air, and was passing on his way to the station.

"Stay!" commanded the other, in a hoarse and unnatural tone.

The face that turned towards him with an air of easy surprise was wonderfully handsome, and now that it recognized an enemy in the man before it, as insolent as handsome.

"Who are you?" inquired Montgomery, in a calmer tone, of which the other possibly failed to note the full significance.

The stranger's answer was to flick the ash from his cigar in the other's face, and then to turn easily and coolly on his heel.

In an instant, Montgomery's hand was on his shoulder, and the two men faced each other at bay.

"You met a lady just now, and you kissed her on leaving?" burst from between Montgomery's white lips.

"I certainly did."

"Do you know who she is?"

"Quite well."

"And you dare to tell me that to my face?"

"Yes, and also to tell you that I hope to meet and kiss the lady a great many more times."

"Never, at least, in this world again," grimly broke in the other, lashed to madness by the insolent smile of his antagonist, and stepping back a pace, he levelled the revolver full at the stranger's face.

As the other saw the gleam of the barrel he shouted "Stay!" and threw back his head, but the action was too late, the bullet struck him in the temple, and he fell to the ground, his face bathed in blood.

For a moment the other stood motionless with the smoking weapon in his hand. Then he stooped and looked in the face of the dead man.

All the amazing fury had died out of his heart; he looked towards the home where his wife was awaiting him, and he murmured, "God forgive you, Alice, you have made me a murderer." Then there came to him, as to all similarly circumstanced, the brute instinct of self-preservation. "No one saw me arrive," he muttered to himself, "no one will suspect me; still, I would like *her* to know that I had found out her crime and punished it."

As he said this, a strange, ghastly smile, weird in the extreme, crept over his face, and he laid on the dead man's breast gently—not in tribute to the man, but in reverence of death—the wedding-ring which he had bought that day to replace the missing one.

"She will understand by this just how it happened," he murmured, as he turned to go.

Once he looked back and saw the dark form lying on the lonely road, and, so strange a composite is humanity, he felt a thrill of revengeful joy, to think how refined a method of punishment he had discovered for his wife.

Poor, short-sighted, misguided man; how little he dreamt of the widespread harm which that small, innocent-looking gold hoop was destined to work.

CHAPTER IV.

THE shriek of the railway whistle recalled George Montgomery to a sense of his desperate situation, and, at the same time, suggested a means of escape. The 8.45 fast up-train was arriving. It was due in New York an hour later. There was the barest possibility that he might be arrested on his arrival in New York, but, on the other hand, the general ignorance as to his having been at the scene of the murder, the distance from the telegraph station, and the infinite advantages presented by the great metropolis for concealing his identity, far out-balanced the possible risk, and the fugitive hesitatingly entered the train.

For the first time in his life he anathemized the long, well-lit cars common to all, and remembered with regret the narrow and private first-class carriages which he had seen on the English railroads. How he would have liked to bury himself between their sheltering cushions, and by means of a handsome fee to the guard have secured the compartment to himself.

Who shall describe what the murderer feels during the first hour of his criminal life, when the crime has been unpremeditated, and there has been no previous process of hardening up? An hour ago this man was one who rightly claimed the respect of all his fellow-men, and had his claim abundantly allowed. *Now* he had fallen, sheer and at a single plunge, through civilization's whole strata of respectability, to find himself jarred and stupefied by the fall on the bed-rock of crime, below which nothing human goes. He picked up a paper lying in the adjoining seat, and his eye caught the heading of a flagrant defalcation unearthed that day. Two hours previous he had read the same news and had felt only contempt for the miserable delinquent; *now* the mere swindler seemed as far removed from him in the category of crime as Lazarus in Heaven seemed removed from Dives in torment.

As the train sped on, the remembrance of his wife's infidelity finally drove all thought of his crime from his mind. As memory, ruthless and unsparing, pictured to his gaze all that they had been to each other, and recalled every incident of their courtship and marriage, when he had so blindly and foolishly thought that they were all the world to each other, the limits of the carriage in which he traveled seemed impossible to hold him, and the old lust of murder crept up on his brain like a returning springtide.

When the fresh paroxysm had spent itself the train entered New York.

Within twenty minutes a carriage stopped at a certain number in Nassau Street, and the fugitive, with the aid of his private key, entered his office. As he did so, the janitor handed him some letters which had arrived since he had left. These he carelessly cast aside, reserving one, the handwriting of which seemed familiar. This he laid on one side. There was no lack of decision in George Montgomery's actions. First of all, he wrote a letter to his partner, saying that circumstances beyond his control compelled his temporary absence, and requesting that until further advised, a certain sum be paid monthly to his wife. He also intimated that he had taken with him a copy of the firm's telegraphic code which he would use if necessary.

After concluding such arrangements as he deemed advisable for the proper conduct of the business during his absence, he withdrew from the safe a considerable sum of money, substituting his check on a leading bank for the same. Then, after ringing for a messenger boy, he ran his fingers through his address-book and having consulted the shipping list to see as to the outgoing vessels, a sudden inspiration seemed to seize him, and he ordered a cab and drove to the private residence of Isamord Hadley, principal owner of the New York & Spanish Steamship Company.

"The tide serves at 3 A.M.," he muttered, as he took his seat in a cab, "and I believe Spain has no extradition treaty with this country, and if she has, no American detective could find me there, so long as I have plenty of money."

To the majority of criminals such a reflection would have been like a reprieve from death, but the brooding brow and leaden eye of this man told that there was no balm in Gilead for his tortured soul, and that wherever he went, and to the last breath of his life, he must carry with him, like an incurable, malignant cancer, the knowledge of a crime, horrifying beyond conception to his mind, and yet unrepented of, because amply justified by the monstrous circumstance of his bride's infidelity. His unbalanced mind inveighed against Heaven for loading him with a trial so far beyond mortal strength or endurance. Like stormy gusts of passion these wild, rebellious thoughts swept across his mind, wrecking and devastating the training of a lifetime as they went, and leaving him faint and breathless with their fury.

During the mental lull which followed one of these outbursts he bethought him of the letter of which the handwriting was familiar. This letter, which he had selected from the others which the janitor had given him, he had placed in his pocket, and he now essayed to open it. The jolting of the cab and the uncertain light of the street, however, made him change his mind, and he returned the letter to his pocket unopened.

Presently the cab stopped and the fugitive alighted. Upon inquiry, he found that his friend was at home and ready to see him. These two men had been bosom friends from their boyhood, and their friendship had in maturer years become intensified and solidified by the fact that they were brother Masons in the same lodge.

Isamord Hadley's face grew white and grave as his friend told him of the events of that terrible evening.

"You surely must be dreaming, George," he said at length, "I have not seen much of your wife, but from what I did see I would pledge my life unhesitatingly on her innocence. For Heaven's sake, man, go back to her."

"Never while I live will I willingly look on her face again." This was said fiercely and with an air of great determination, but with a quiver in the brusqueness of his voice, and then the poor tortured soul turned his head to hide the great sobs which now shook his frame. The kindly voice and the sympathetic eye of his old friend had, for the time being, exorcised the demon of jealousy, and now poor George Montgomery stood revealed a most miserable, broken-hearted man.

"You forget the murder," at length he faltered; "how could I ever go back?"

Two hours later Mr. Hadley left his house in company with George Montgomery in disguise. A cab took them to the docks, and when they stepped on board the "City of Seville" Montgomery was introduced to the Captain as Mr. Angus Forman, a citizen of Chicago bound for Cadiz. As owner of the vessel, Mr. Hadley bespoke for his friend every kind attention and assistance which the captain and officers could render him. Before leaving he took an opportunity of explaining to the captain that his friend's journey was partly undertaken on account of his health, which had become impaired through over-work, and partly through a recent family trouble, the details of which he did not enter into.

At 3.15 A.M. the "City of Seville" raised her anchor and left her moorings, and when the early summer's morning dawned, she was fast leaving the land behind her.

As the outline of the shore grew dim, the solitary passenger on board the "City of Seville" strained his gaze to catch the latest glimpse of land, and the summons of the steward to breakfast fell unheeded on his ears. At length, when the haze hid the land from view, and only the heaving billows met his eye on every side, he turned away.

Half an hour later the captain on the bridge saw the figure of a man fall prone on deck. The occurrence was unusual, and the captain left his post to ascertain what it meant. He found his guest, Mr. Angus Forman, lying insensible with an open letter tightly grasped in his hand. By the captain's orders, the passenger was removed to his cabin, where he shortly afterwards regained consciousness. As sensibility returned, his first gaze was directed to the letter, which was still clenched, all crumpled, in his stiffened grasp.

"Oh, unhappy wretch that I am, and more than murderer," he moaned. "My poor, faithful darling, I have killed your brother and now you must loathe me forevermore. Oh, why did I leave that cursed ring there to establish my guilt!" As the wailing died from his lips, he turned from the light as a creature stricken to death retreats to the darkest corner of its lair to die in.

That night the strange passenger of the "City of Seville" was raving in delirium, and for weeks, while the sailing vessel ploughed on its monotonous way, he lay between life and death.

At length there came a day when the watchers by the invalid's side surrendered all hope, and it was then that, for the first time, the captain felt it incumbent upon him to read the letter which had apparently precipitated the catastrophe.

In itself the letter gave little clue to the secret of his passenger, but coupled with the latter's incoherent ravings, the captain was able to arrive at a fairly accurate knowledge of what the secret was.

The letter was addressed to George Montgomery and was evidently from his wife's grandmother. In it the writer intimated that her grand-daughter, through dread that it might lessen her husband's love for her, had concealed from him the fact that she had a scapegrace brother. The old lady thought that *any* secret between husband and wife was harmful, and in that belief she had thought it best to make him acquainted with the fact, so that he might find some opportunity to pave the way towards inviting his wife's full confidence, and so remove what might be a future cause of grave misunderstanding. "I am the more anxious to set you two right on this matter," she continued, "because I feel that sooner or later you will yourself hear of my wretched grandson from outside sources, and if the indications are correct, sooner rather than later, as he is again in some trouble or other, and likely to come for help to his sister, as he has been in the habit of doing. It seemed to me that I saw him lurking about our house to-day, but my eyesight is very indifferent and I cannot speak positively as to this." The letter concluded with an urgent appeal to him to remember his wife's sensitiveness of mind as well as her delicacy of constitution, and to invite and not force her confidence.

After he had finished the letter, the captain looked at the name on the envelope. He was a self-contained, trustworthy man, and beyond a prolonged "Ah—h," as he noted the discrepancy between the names of Montgomery and Forman, he gave no utterance to his feelings, as he passed to his cabin, where he again sealed up the passenger's letter and addressed it (Mr. Angus Forman).

At midnight the captain was summoned to the sick man's side.

"He is sinking fast," explained the first officer in a low tone, "but he is conscious at last, and wishes to see you."

CHAPTER V.

AS Alice Montgomery was returning to the house from the peach walk, where she had met her brother according to his appointment, she caught a glimpse of her husband hastily entering the wood. He was walking fast, and before she had decided to call to him he had entered the wood and was lost to her sight.

"He is searching for me," she murmured, pleased at his apparent precipitancy, and yet a little anxious as to how she was to explain her failure to meet him. As she followed him into the wood her steps grew slower as she found herself unable to frame to her entire satisfaction an excuse for her very glaring omission.

"He must have gone to the Lake Summer-House, thinking to find me there," she presently surmised, as she came to two cross forest paths. Saying this she entered the road opposite to that which her husband had taken. When she reached the Summer-House and found it empty, a look of alarm for the first time crossed her face.

"Oh, I hope he has not met Tom," she whispered to herself half in dismay. At that instant a shot rang through the wood, startling her almost into a cry. "I wonder what that can be," she exclaimed, "George has no fire-arms; but perhaps it is some one shooting at the squirrels."

After a moment's hesitation she retraced her steps towards the direction of the report, and passed into the foot-path taken by her husband some ten minutes previously.

This brought her to the turnpike road, which was deserted, but for an object lying on the ground some fifty yards away, and not clearly discernible at that distance in the fading light.

A strange tremor filled her breast and almost palsied her limbs as she moved towards the inanimate object lying so still and awful; and now as she neared it, fast taking the semblance of a human body.

There are moments whose experience no pen can describe, and far be it from us to attempt the impossible. What of agony and horror Alice Montgomery suffered when she saw her brother lying dead on the public highway, while his parting kiss was yet warm on her lips, to be understood must be endured. Her first impulse was to give way to her uncontrollable grief; but at that instant her straining eyes caught sight of an object which froze the first cry on her lips. This was the new wedding-ring which shone cold and distinct against the dark coat worn by the dead man. As it lay there it seemed to voice the full intent with which the murderer had placed it on his victim's breast.

As if carved in pale cold marble the young bride stood there staring at the dead body, and at the awful ring shrieking out its horrid tale. So silent and still she stood that the birds fluttered near to her on the road, and the squirrels stopped midway in their flight, and sat upright in the dusty way to regard her.

Then, like a statue endowed with vitality, she stooped and removed the ring from its place, murmuring in a low monotone, "The ring he bought for me to-day." Then she looked at it strangely and almost coldly, and finally placed it in her pocket-book. Only a little shiver and a gasp disturbed the calm—that was all.

With a desperate effort and with a self-possession bordering on the horrible, she removed the revolver, of which the handle was discernible, from the dead man's pocket, and peered into each separate chamber. Alas! they were all full. For an instant the long white fingers grasped the weapon and then a cartridge driven from its place fell into her palm. This she also placed in her pocket-book. Then she stooped and picked up the empty shell which the murderer had cast from his revolver after firing. Would it fit her brother's weapon? It did; the pistols were of the same (Smith & Wesson) make and also of similar calibre.

Her next task was a still more terrible one, but it was

performed without a tremor of the quick and capable fingers. With gentle yet unfaltering touch she took the match-box from her brother's vest pocket, and, having abstracted a single match from it, she returned it to its place. Then, moving into the shadow of the wood, lest the flame should attract attention, she applied the lighted match to the empty chamber, smoking and discoloring it as if the pistol had been recently fired.

This done, she laid the revolver close to the outstretched hand of the dead man.

"God forgive me," she said in a low tone, "for making my brother a suicide, but it is to save my husband's life."

This was said with the same unnatural calm, and then the speaker knelt beside the dead man and kissed him on the lips which were still unchilled by death. Once, twice, three times, her lips, colder than those of the dead, sought his face, then she took out her handkerchief to wipe the blood which was penetrating the poor, unseeing, wide-open eyes. Then, remembering the part which she had to play, she refrained.

"God help me, my deceit has killed my brother; I must try to save my husband." Murmuring this she turned from the dreadful spectacle on the road and passed into the wood with a strange mechanical woodenness of step, as if the shock which had spared her brain and hands had benumbed or paralyzed her lower limbs.

As she neared the house her grandfather rose from his seat on the piazza, and advanced to meet her.

"What is the matter, child?" he cried, alarmed beyond measure at the ghastly face on which the seal of a great horror had been stamped, and alarmed no less at the unnatural calm of his grand-daughter's manner, as she stood before him with staring eyes, whose dilated pupils suggested insanity.

"Grandpapa, go down to the road," she murmured pantingly, and with a strange catch in her voice, "down by the white elm tree; something terrible has happened to Tom." And, her gruesome work being ended, poor over-spent nature gave way, and she fell unconscious to the ground.

When she had been restored to sensibility and carried to her room, her grandfather, calling the colored butler to follow him, went to investigate the cause of her emotion. The gardener, who was found watering the plants in the front, was also summoned to accompany his master.

What the three found the reader already knows. The old white-haired grandfather uttered no sound, and only the exclamations of the horrified servants broke the weird silence.

"A lamp and a stretcher, Julius, quick!" exclaimed the old man, silencing with a wave of his hand the lamentations of the others. Then he stooped and put his ear to the chest of the silent figure; long and patiently he listened, and then, as if reluctant to believe the worst, or still uncertain, he undid the coat and vest and re-applied his ear to catch the faintest flicker of life, if it be that any such were left in the prostrate body.

"Your ear is younger than mine, try whether you can hear any action in his heart." This was said to the butler, who bent his head in silent obedience to the commands of his master.

"Seems to me that I can hear *something*, sah!"

The minutes appeared hours while the two waited in the gathering gloom for the return of Julius with the lamp and the stretcher. At last, however, he arrived, and the inanimate body was carried gently to the house. Five minutes later a mounted groom left for the nearest doctor. When the latter had made his examination he announced that life was not extinct, and that while it hung by a thread, there was still room for hope. The bullet had fractured the skull and caused concussion of the brain, but the latter organ had not been penetrated, the missile having glanced from the bone in consequence of the slanting position of the forehead at the moment of fire.

"I think it right to tell you," the doctor said at parting, "that while the patient's life may possibly be saved, his reason will probably be endangered. Do you think the young man intended to commit suicide?" he added by way of inquiry, as his last remark was received in silence.

"I think not," was the reply; "he was full of life, and was constantly getting into trouble, but nothing weighed heavily on his mind; no, I imagine that he took out his revolver to fire at some over-bold squirrel, perhaps, and while examining the chambers to see whether they were all loaded he probably touched the hair-trigger unintentionally; I think that is, perhaps, the correct solution of the mystery."

"I have no doubt that it is," said the doctor, as he turned to go. "Good-night, sir."

CHAPTER VI.

WHEN the young bride, Alice Montgomery, pale and wan, the mere spectre of her former self, left the sick room for the first time, a month had elapsed from the date of the events narrated in the last chapter. The interval had brought no tidings of her missing husband, beyond the intelligence conveyed by his partner that he had visited the office on the night of his departure, and arranged for her maintenance during a prolonged absence. This uncertainty as to his fate had greatly retarded her recovery, and the triumph which her youth had thus gained in dragging her back to life was, as yet, too uncertain to mitigate the anxiety felt by her aged relatives. Her brother had recovered from his wound, and had, in a measure, regained his health, but the mental disorder predicted by the medical adviser was now only too apparent. Of the occurrences of that dreadful night he had evidently no recollection, and he never spoke of them. His mind seemed perpetually occupied with monetary troubles, and no assurance on the part of his grandfather that these had all been adjusted served to allay his apprehension. From a youthful irrational creature of erratic habits he seemed suddenly to have passed into careworn middle life, burdened with a thousand gloomy anxieties.

Altogether the house of Arlington lay in a sombre shadow during those bright summer days, and many silvery hairs were added to its aged heads in the long weeks of trouble and grief through which they had to pass.

"Grandma, have you got my purse?" suddenly asked the young bride, while seated on the veranda one afternoon in the early days of her convalescence.

"Yes, dear," replied the other, a delicate flush mantling her cheeks as she thought of its contents—the cartridge and the wedding-ring; "shall I fetch it?"

"Please, dear; has anyone else seen it, grannie?"

"No, love; I have kept it locked up since the night of the

—the accident."

No more passed between these two on the subject, but each understood the other, and if the gloom did not lighten with the mutual understanding, their hearts grew stronger to endure its burden.

"Why do you not wear your wedding-ring?" her grandmother inquired one day.

"I lost it the morning George left."

A look of perplexity crossed the other's face, but the trouble in her grand-daughter's eyes checked further inquiry.

When the "City of Seville" sailed into the port of Cadiz the captain of the vessel handed a sealed envelope to his passenger, Angus Forman, with the assurance, somewhat stiffly delivered, that his secret, whatever it might be, was safe with him.

The other received the envelope in silence, and when he broke the seal and found the letter from his wife's grandmother, which had been the means of revealing his victim's identity, he read it again without apparent emotion.

During the long weeks of delirium and slow recovery to health in which he had passed the interval of the sailing vessel's slow passage, he had discounted all human misery it seemed to him, and as he stood on the deck, the mere skeleton of his former self, he felt alike indifferent to the approach of weal or woe.

Far down in his breast there ached the dull ceaseless pain of a love forever lost, which drowned every other feeling and made him indifferent to it.

When the custom-house officers came aboard he was surprised—after a languid fashion, and as one thinking of some casual acquaintance rather than himself—that no detectives accompanied them, and that he was not arrested for murder, but when he found that no inquiry was made for him, and he was at liberty to go and come as he pleased, there was no corresponding relief or elation visible in his manner.

On bidding the captain adieu he thanked him for his great kindness. "I owe you my life," he remarked, "and when I am certain that I am grateful to you for preserving it, I will thank you more warmly," with which enigmatical sentence he passed ashore.

As health returned his tortured mind sought relief in excitement and he left Cadiz for Madrid, where he strove to allay the grief which gnawed at his heart by plunging into the wild excitement of that hot-headed and hot-blooded capital. After a time the ferocious excitement of the weekly bull fight ceased to deaden the agony which preyed at his heart, and he allied himself with a revolutionary movement, which had the advantage of promising equal excitement with some risk to the life which had long been a burden to him.

The Carlist rising seemed like the first glimpse of Heaven's good will to him, and as such he embraced the opportunity it afforded. The contagious excitement aroused by the Pretender, thrilled through his being, and, at length, he opened his soul to his fellow-men. It were more correct, perhaps, to say fellow-man, since his sole companion and confidant was a much-travelled Spanish soldier of fortune, whose desperate circumstances, as narrated by himself, had first melted the icy reserve which begirt the heart-sore wanderer.

As the two travelled together to the front, the stranger, by insidious inquiries gathered piecemeal George Montgomery's history. More particularly, however, he seemed interested in the bulky telegraphic code which the other carried with him, and he was puzzled, he said, with his eternal smile, to understand how a book of the kind could be of any practical value; he appeared to be unlettered in business ways, and the other, to while away the long evenings, explained to him the working of the code, as he would have elucidated any ordinary puzzle.

"It seems plain to you, doesn't it?" said his friend, one

night, laughingly, as he clasped his head in his palms at the end of a long explanation, "yet I swear the whole thing is Greek to me. I suppose my brain must be unusually dense."

That night a false alarm was given, and, in the confusion, George Montgomery was parted from his friend. When order was at length restored, and the former endeavored to collect his baggage, he found that his telegraphic cipher was missing. A hasty march was made from the dangerous locality, and in the darkness he was parted from his friend, whom he did not see again. "It is the fortune of war," he remarked, somewhat bitterly to himself, for he had grown to like his new-found friend, and in the daily exigencies of an exciting life he soon forgot his passing acquaintance.

The date of this alarm was the 5th of August. On the 10th the firm of Alford & Montgomery, in New York, received a cable message in cipher, of which the translation was:

"Please remit by cable to the Bank of Madrid, five thousand dollars, payable to my order without identification.

"George Montgomery."

On receipt of this despatch the firm telegraphed to Mrs. Montgomery, and received in reply a request to assure her husband that all was well, and to beg him to return to his wife without delay.

On the evening of the 10th, the Atlantic cable carried the following message in cipher:

"We have remitted five thousand dollars, by cable, as requested. Your wife entreats you to return, and says, 'All is well.'

"Alford & Montgomery."

When this message was delivered and translated, the receiver smiled strangely as he lit a fresh cigar, adding, after he had established its fire, "Seeing how easy it has been, I'm only sorry, friend Montgomery, that I did not cable for twenty thousand dollars instead of five thousand dollars. It was a bright idea to steal that very useful code of yours."

At that moment the clank of a heavy sabre on the marble floor of the hotel smote on his ear, and the weight of a heavy hand fell on his shoulder.

"I arrest you, señor, at the instance of the Bank of Madrid."

"The charge?" fiercely ejaculated the other, finding his struggles useless.

"Forgery," was the grim and laconic reply.

"Ah, well, that is an old hallucination of the bank's and easily answered; let me light a cigarette any way," urged the other, with simulated indifference, as he turned the folded dispatch towards the light. The officer made no objection and presently his prisoner ground the ashes of the telegraphic message beneath his heel.

At Arlington, Alice Montgomery waited with agonizing anxiety for a cabled reply to the loving message which she had sent across the ocean to her unhappy husband. As the days passed without bringing her any answering message she persuaded her husband's partner to telegraph again to Madrid. Still no response, and still another message sped on its way beneath the ocean, only, however, to result in the same stony silence.

At length, in reply to a letter sent to the Bank of Madrid, there came the intelligence that the $5,000 remitted had never been applied for, and that the Cable Company had only been able to deliver the first message, all the others being still at the hotel where the husband had received the first one.

Perhaps the information that her husband had received the loving message which she had sent him, and had closed his ears and his heart to her piteous appeal, was the bitterest drop in the cup of Mrs. Montgomery's affliction; and for a while it seemed as if in grinding out the ashes of the cablegram beneath his heel in the hotel at Madrid, the villain who had stolen George Montgomery's cipher, had likewise ground out the life of his now thoroughly heartbroken wife. But no thought of compunction crossed the mind of the felon, now languishing in a Spanish cell and torturing his mind how best he could manage to get hold of that money in the bank, so that with a portion of it he might bribe his jailers and regain his freedom.

"I wonder how my American friend enjoys fighting the Spanish troops?" he smilingly queried of himself one day as he sat under the great white-washed wall of the prison court rolling a fresh cigarette.

At that moment, George Montgomery, sorely wounded, was bleeding his life out on the sunny slopes of the Sierra Morena mountains, and murmuring brokenly, now faintly, now passionately, as his fever ebbed and flowed, the name of his dearly loved wife, whom fate had at last, to all appearances, forever separated from him.

CHAPTER VII.

IN a Spanish monastery George Montgomery recovered from the wounds which had so nearly proved fatal, and, by-and-by, when the last gleanings of the autumnal crop of grapes shrivelled on its southern walls, he felt the dawnings of returning convalescence.

As his eye, released from the shadow of death, swept the panorama of mountain ranges and smiling valleys visible from his lofty eyrie in the monastery, earth seemed very fair to him, and the life, so hardly retained, acquired a double value in his sight.

His mind, with recovering strength, began to regain its equilibrium, and his disordered brain was at last able to review in proper perspective the situation as between himself and (first) his wife and (second) his crime.

As his thoughts, purged from the dross of passion in that habitation where nothing unworthy could live, calmly reviewed the situation, he felt abased to think how selfishly he had acted — how cowardly indeed, he thought, as he scourged himself with bitter self-recriminations.

Clear to him it seemed, as the evening star which rose on his view nightly and darkened every other constellation by its brilliancy, that his duty was to have communicated with his wife on the first available moment after learning of the horrible mistake he had made in assuming her brother to be her lover; and this he ought to have done at all hazards to himself.

Was it too late? What might not have happened in those months of silence?

These questions tortured his mind day by day with ever-increasing violence, and finally, and reluctantly, the holy brotherhood permitted the departure of the wounded man in order to enable him, while yet perhaps there was time, to make atonement for a grievous wrong.

He bade the monks adieu with unfeigned regret. The

odor of sanctity which seemed to pervade the very walls of the monastery had impressed him powerfully; he had seen how, while ministering to human trouble and endowed with broad human sympathies, the brothers still held themselves "unspotted from the world," and he felt, on bidding them farewell, like an African traveler, who, driven by desperate circumstances, leaves behind him the last well and the last glimpse of verdure to plunge into the unknown and illimitable desert beyond, strewn with the skeletons of those who have gone before.

He shuddered at times when he reflected what possibly awaited him as he remembered that awful figure lying on the cold road with the night descending on it like a pall. He shuddered but he did not hesitate. The monastic teachings had cleared his brain and outlined a path which he had determined to follow, if his life lasted, until he reached the desired goal.

He still had ample funds in his possession, and he was accordingly able to reach Cadiz without delay. Immediately on arriving he wrote a long letter to his wife, explaining fully the circumstances under which he had fled; he concealed nothing: it was part of his merited punishment he felt (and that not the least painful) to be compelled to make the humiliating confession to his wife that he had suspected her fidelity even during their honeymoon.

The writing of this letter was a terrible ordeal and called into distressing activity the keenest emotions.

Never perhaps had the reasons for utter despair taken such palpable shape as when the closing lines of his own letter lay before him in all their stern significance.

"I shall never cease to love you while life lasts," these said, "but I know that I can now awake in you only feelings of abhorrence as the murderer of your brother. I will not try to see you again, for indeed I think that one glance of reproach from your eyes would kill me outright where I stood.

"I am leaving this city within twenty-four hours not to

return. I cannot give you my address and I would not if I could. I have only one request to make, that you will endeavor to blot all recollection of my most unhappy self from your mind. And even that miserable solace is, I feel, to be denied me, for however time might efface all memory of me as a husband, eternity itself could not obliterate the horrible recollection of me as your brother's murderer."

The following day, when the "City of Havana" sailed for Cuba, George Montgomery (or rather Angus Forman, for he had resumed his assumed name), was one of the passengers.

Why he had made the West Indies his objective point he might perhaps have been unable truthfully to decide. The reason that he gave to himself was that his mind required yet another change of scene, while his enfeebled body demanded that it should be to a still warmer clime. Deep down in his heart, however, he was conscious of another reason, a craving or soul-hunger to be nearer the Mecca of his heart. He fought in vain against the tumultuous joy which swelled in his breast when an inward voice whispered day by day and louder and louder as the vessel surged on its way, "half-way home," and yet he told himself with a despair to which each breath of hope added keener poignancy, that the second half of that way his feet would never traverse.

On the fifth day out from Cadiz, an event occurred which had considerable effect on his after life. As he stood on the deck listlessly watching a school of porpoises which had raced alongside the ship, he was conscious of a considerable commotion among the sailors. The cause was the discovery of a stowaway among the merchandise in the hold. As the wretched prisoner was dragged forward for the captain's inspection, Montgomery recognized in him his old companion, the Spanish soldier of fortune, De Leon, who had disappeared on the night of the alarm when they were on their way to join the forces of

Don Carlos. To the readers this enterprising gentleman is known as the man who stole the telegraphic cipher, who used it to cable for $5,000, and who finally wound up in a Spanish prison before his roguery was consummated to his satisfaction.

By appealing to the cupidity of his jailer, he had at last induced the latter to secure a temporary substitute and leave of absence for a few hours from the jail in order to obtain the money from the bank which the latter had been instructed to pay over to George Montgomery on demand.

He had gone to the bank under the keen surveillance of his confederate, the jailer, only to find, however, that the advice to pay the money had been cancelled.

This was a death-blow to his hopes, but the hardy villain, surmising that liberty even without wealth was better than incarceration, determined to make a bold dash for liberty while he had the chance.

Watching his opportunity he tripped up his disappointed and now furious companion, the jailer, with such violence as to rob that baffled functionary of what little intelligence he possessed, for the space of several minutes. De Leon's knowledge of the purlieus of Madrid enabled him to hide in safety until a suitable opportunity arose for him to leave the city, and through his ingenuity as an adventurer, he was able to reach the coast in safety. There, after a time, he had been able to secrete himself on board the "City of Havana" while the careless sailors were enjoying their afternoon siesta.

On board this Spanish ship the captain's views of a stowaway's crime were, to say the least, somewhat harsh.

The wretched man's starved condition and the misery of his appearance aroused no spark of pity in the breast of the unfeeling skipper, whose moustache bristled with rage at the thought of the daring and effrontery of the man who had perpetrated such a fraud upon him and the owners of the ship.

"Fifty lashes on the bare back at once, and to be handed

over to the authorities in Havana on landing," was the sentence decreed, with the accompaniment of many elaborate and inspiring Castilian oaths by the haughty Spaniard. His desperate situation paralyzed the stowaway into silence. One glance at the ruthless face of the captain satisfied the poor wretch, whose career as an adventurer enabled him to read the human countenance like an open page, that appeal was hopeless, while of means of escape there were none, with only the wide waste of waters as a refuge.

As the hunted gaze of the captive scanned all the faces around him he suddenly drew back as if struck in the face by a blow, and cast his eyes downward to the deck. He had recognized George Montgomery. In an instant he summed up the situation in this wise: "If this man identifies me I shall be handed over to the authorities at Havana, not as a suspicious character, but as a thief and a forger, and that, added to my conspiracy with the jailer and my escape, will ensure me twenty years of the galleys."

As these thoughts crashed like a shell through De Leon's brain, he forgot about the flogging which he was going to receive; the enormity of the terrible punishment awaiting him in Spain obliterating every other thought. All his native hardihood had deserted him, and he hung limp and with closed eyes against the mast to which he had been lashed in readiness for the ordered whipping.

He was vaguely conscious of a sudden silence among the men around him, and, at length opening his eyes fearfully, he saw Montgomery in conversation with the captain, and pointing towards him. He saw, or at least concluded, that his worst fears had been realized; that the man he had robbed had recognized him, and as he fancied he could hear him detailing the particulars of his crime, he closed his eyes hurriedly and the pallor on his face whitened to the hue of death.

In his conclusion that Montgomery had recognized him

the miserable culprit was correct, but as the reader is aware, the former had no cognizance of his theft or of his other attempted frauds, and his conversation with the captain at the moment was simply a proposition to pay double compensation to the ship's owners for the fare of which they had been defrauded, together with a handsome *douceur* to the captain himself for the liberation of the prisoner.

The captain listened in moody silence, but under his lids an avaricious gleam shot outwards and downwards. "Captain! he is an old fellow-traveler of mine, and a right good fellow; let him go; if you had ever seen him as I have seen him in good circumstances, you would be shocked at the change in his appearance; he has suffered enough already, God knows."

This appeal moved the captain not one whit, but it provided a way for him to secure the proffered consideration, and the grimness of his features relaxed as if the other had released him from a disagreeable and painful duty from which naturally his whole soul revolted.

"Say no more, señor, your assurance as to that unfortunate gentleman's respectability is received unreservedly. I can, of course, accept nothing for myself; the knowledge that I have been of service to you is in itself sufficient reward (this with a profound bow and radiant smile), but my duty to the owners of the ship compels me to accept your offer to recoup us for this man's passage money. If, however, you will see the purser, these details can be readily arranged. I will instruct him to receive the money;" whereupon the captain left for the purser's office.

When George Montgomery had settled accounts with the purser, he had not only paid double fare for his erring friend, but he had, in response to a somewhat broad hint from the purser, paid a further sum of $250, which the latter intimated would be the probable fine imposed on the captain if it were discovered by the owners that he had not inflicted the usual punishment on the stowaway. Perhaps it was to avoid the possibility of the owners discovering such a flagrant dereliction of duty that no entries were made in the ship's books of the sums handed over that day!

When George Montgomery returned on deck, he found the inanimate figure of his old fellow-traveler still bound to the mast. In response to his glance of surprise at the captain, the latter explained with a smile and another overpowering bow, that he thought Señor Forman might like to release the prisoner himself.

Accepting a knife tendered by one of the crew he advanced to the mast. The sight of the pale and haggard features covered with the glassy moisture of a sudden and unspeakable terror might have moved a heart of stone. The heavy lids still tightly closed the horrified eyes, and the whole aspect was that of the dead.

"I have come to release you," George whispered in his ear, but the other gave no sign, save only that a dark flush began to creep up over his neck.

"Don't you remember me, old friend? Great Heavens, a glass of brandy here, quick! The man is dying!"

The eyes had opened wide and stared horribly while you might count five, and the fugitive color had died suddenly away and the body fallen a dead weight on the ropes.

But "good news never kills," and at length the sorrowful knight of fortune recovered consciousness to find himself alone with the friend whom he had wronged, and who was now bending over him in eager solicitude. His bonds had been removed and he lay in his friend's cabin. When he had satisfied himself that he was not the victim of some pleasing hallucination, and that he was really at liberty, he took his friend's hand between both his own, and kissed it again and again, while the hot tears rained unheeded from his poor eyes.

"Ah, you are very weak," explained his friend, "but here comes the cook with some nice nourishing soup."

CHAPTER VIII.

GEORGE MONTGOMERY took an early opportunity of explaining to his friend De Leon, that, for certain reasons, he was traveling under an assumed name. To the other, it is lamentable to add, this appeared the most natural thing in the world, and he never gave the matter a second thought.

The devotion of the rescued stowaway to the friend who had saved him was touching in the extreme. He followed him like his shadow, with a dog-like fidelity which awoke the sneers of the supercilious Spaniards. There were occasions when these sneers roused the ire of the patient De Leon and prompt retribution seemed very near the heads of the offenders, but the butt of their shafts recollected himself in time and dissembled his wrath, conscious that he was not yet quite out of danger, and that so long as he was on board ship and within touch, he was by no means beyond the reach of Spanish malice.

At length the island of Cuba was reached, and the two friends left the ship in safety.

On the night of their arrival, as the two were seated in the Hotel Pasaje, in Havana, the second officer of the ship, who had been celebrating his return with some old friends, entered the hotel. When he saw De Leon, he pointed him out jeeringly to the friends who accompanied him, as "the stowaway."

He had been a special offender in this respect on board ship, so that it scarcely needed the fresh insult to fire De Leon's blood.

When the latter noticed that the officer's companions were regarding him curiously, he rose to his feet with much deliberation, and, lifting his full wine-glass from the table, he threw its contents straight into the officer's face. As the latter endeavored to wipe the dark claret from his face, De Leon, with the air of a grandee of Spain, raised his hat to the other gentleman; then fixing his gaze on the officer, he said; "I am at your service, señor."

The interposition of the hotel officials prevented any continuation of the quarrel there, and the entire party left together. George Montgomery, who accompanied his friend, was in dismay at the quarrel and the duel with the officer which seemed impending.

"You do not know, my friend, what you are about. If you knew what it was to have blood on your hands you would die rather than shed it."

The other glanced at him strangely for a moment, and then replied, "In anything but this I would obey you willingly, but I am by birth a Spanish noble, and this man has insulted me. I have avenged that insult, and now I should be a coward if I did not give him the satisfaction he requires."

At this moment one of the officer's friends approached Montgomery and informed him courteously that the gentleman who had been insulted demanded satisfaction, and intimated that the more promptly it could be afforded, the more it would be to the taste of his principal.

As George Montgomery hesitated and then protested that nothing would induce him to sanction a duel, De Leon took the matter into his own hands, and said, "This gentleman is the only friend I have in the city; he will not act, therefore I must dispense with a second, and I say I am ready now to meet your principal. I have no preference as to weapons, but as the choice rests with me, and to save time, I name the rapier. I am content to accompany you alone, and as soon as we can secure the weapons, I will go with you and settle the matter."

The other bowed gravely, and, promising to return in a few minutes, he left.

"Good-bye, for the present, at least," exclaimed De Leon with outstretched hand to his friend, as his opponent's second returned with the rapiers under his arm. "If all goes well I will return to the hotel in a couple of hours, and if not, why then dearest of friends, adieu," and he raised the other's hand to his lips and kissed it, not formally, but tenderly and even passionately.

"Oh! I cannot let you go alone," returned the other. "It is all wrong, I know, and can only build up untold misery in the future, but I cannot turn my back on a friend."

In reply De Leon pressed his hand, and together they entered one of three carriages which had been summoned for the use of the party.

A drive of twenty minutes landed them on a lonely spot hedged in on three sides by lofty palms and a dense undergrowth of palmetto, and on the other side by the blue waters of the bay, where a solitary craft lay moored near the shore.

The moon was high in the heavens, and the light was almost as clear as day.

When De Leon ran his fingers over the weapon which was handed to him, he seemed jubilant with gaiety. "My friend," he exclaimed, "if I thought I was going to die, I would make a confession to you; I did you a great wrong once. But I shall spit that wretch like a lark, and I cannot afford to lose your friendship, so my confession must wait."

While the preliminary arrangements were being made the movement on shore had attracted the attention of the look-out on board the low-lying craft at anchor a few hundred yards away, and presently a boat put off from the ship containing the three officers on duty, who correctly surmised the cause of the unwonted gathering and came ashore to see the fight.

As they joined the group they saluted its members courteously, but carelessly, as men who were seldom wont to crave permission for their presence, and were indifferent whether it was accorded or not, an impression which was heightened by a certain swagger in their manner which savored more of the buccaneer than of the naval officer, and also by a superfluity of armament about their persons.

When the duellists had taken their places the contrast in

the expressions of the two principals was very marked.

On De Leon's face there was an air of smiling assurance which seemed to goad his opponent almost to fury. He had fully regained his strength during the weeks which had elapsed since his discovery on board ship as a stowaway, and the muscular neck and powerful arms promised that, given equal skill, the observant moon would have left her proud elevation in the sky before his physical powers would surrender to mere fatigue.

At last the signal of attack was given and the fine steel blades slid along each other see-saw as their owners felt their way to the attack. Then the officer shot out his weapon apparently full at the broad breast of his antagonist. But no harm was done, and the ring of the steel hilts as they clashed together, was the only sound which was borne on the night air. A temporary lock of blades prevented any harm being done, and when they were disengaged the two began afresh the see-sawing with their weapons.

De Leon, however, had already gauged his opponent's ability, and before the latter could fathom his intention or do anything beyond blindly advancing his weapon, the other's rapier had disengaged itself from his blade, slid like a lightning flash over his arm and pierced his neck.

The fight was over almost ere the weapon was withdrawn, and the officer, choked with blood, staggered backwards and fell into the arms of his friends.

At that instant a shrill double whistle of warning was heard from the ship and the three officers belonging to it retraced their steps rapidly to the boat. At the same moment a body of Spanish troops plunged through the palmetto, cutlass in hand.

"Stay!" shouted De Leon to the retreating officers, "take us with you."

His suspicious brain had surmised a trap, and he was afraid of the troops as foes. The law and order of Spain he dreaded as much as suspected Christians in former ages feared the Inquisition.

The reasons which impelled the officers to consent to his request may probably be found in the fact that both looked able, powerful men, and one at least had just proved himself to be a very efficient swordsman.

"All right, in with you—quick!" shouted the first officer by way of reply, and the two took their seats hurriedly in the boat, which was immediately pushed off from the shore.

The vessel was found on a closer acquaintance to be engaged in the contraband trade, and the captain in command, in consideration of the sum of two hundred and fifty dollars, agreed to land the two passengers on the mainland of Florida. The arrangement suited his own purposes for the moment although he would have preferred to retain his passengers, and the two were accordingly landed in safety at Punta Rassa, where they engaged a boat and its owner, a Florida oyster dredger of villainous appearance, and, had they known it, of still more evil reputation.

With this man they entered into a contract to take them through the great Lake Okeechobee, with which he assured them he was familiar, and thence northward through the chain of canals and lakes which led to within reasonable distance of one of the principal termini of the very limited railway service of Florida.

Why did George Montgomery choose such a route?

He would probably have found it hard to furnish a reasonable explanation. When he landed in the State it seemed sufficient rapture for the moment to feel that he was once more on the same continent with his wife, and that no terrible width of ocean any longer divided them.

Still he could not forget that he was a fugitive from justice, and that in all probability the "hue and cry" had been raised against him as the murderer of his brother-in-law. He shuddered as he thought that on his first visit to a railway station he might be confronted by a reward offered for his own apprehension.

And so, satisfied with the thought that day by day he was creeping or drifting nearer to the woman for whom his whole soul and body hankered, he seemed to find a temporary contentment in his lot.

His preoccupation of mind rendered him the most unsuspicious of mortals, and so hastened a catastrophe which came near terminating prematurely his wanderings.

In taking a bundle of papers from his pocket one day a package of notes of large denomination fell to the bottom of the boat. As a matter of fact the parcel represented five thousand dollars, and with a five-hundred-dollar bill as its outward symbol looked, it must be confessed, its full value.

As the eyes of the boatman fell upon the parcel they glared at it with a greed of covetousness which De Leon read at a glance and carefully noted. The owner of the notes neither saw nor recked of the commotion aroused by his carelessness. De Leon, however, not only saw the error, but made it quite clear to the boatman that he understood him.

"Ah! my dear friend, there is trouble for us both ahead," De Leon muttered, as he softly soaked the boatman's cartridges in the limpid waters of Lake Okeechobee while that worthy slept. "I," he resumed, "am a Soldier of Fortune, *you*, my worthy ruffian, are simply a murderer! but beware, De Leon watches!"

As he referred to himself as a Soldier of Fortune, it is possible that he was endeavoring to discriminate to the satisfaction of his conscience between a genius of *la haute finance*, who, in extremity, and with the touch of a master, borrows a telegraphic cipher and uses it with brilliant, if ephemeral, result, and a simple highway robber.

It is but just, however, to the brave De Leon to say that his cheeks tingled with shame whenever he thought of the very scurvy trick he had once played on his old and unsuspecting friend in stealing his code and suppressing the message from his wife.

"Ah! it is a sorry business to rob a whole-souled generous man who trusts you blindly."

As De Leon reflected thus, the boat lay at anchor for the night on the broad bosom of that inland sea, Lake Okeechobee.

"I think," he whispered to himself, "I ought to mention that message to my friend; it might lessen his distress, and yet how *can* I let him know how I have wronged him and tried to defraud him? I cannot do it."

Three weeks later they stopped at a landing-place on the Kissimmee River, in order to secure some fresh food. They had passed through the great lake in safety, and also through its principal tributary to a point north of Fort Kissimmee. That stoppage was the first of any consequence since they had left Lake Okeechobee, and it is possible that the careful watch observed by De Leon having been without result up to that time, his vigils had grown somewhat careless.

This, however, is mere conjecture, but on the night of that landing, De Leon awoke from a heavy stupor to find the boatman raising his axe to slay his friend Montgomery. De Leon essayed to rise to his feet, yelling out an alarm to his friend as he did so. The assassin, however, had taken the precaution to tie some ropes across the other's limbs, loosely enough so as not to awake him, yet in such a way as to prevent him rendering any sudden assistance to his friend.

The immediate result of De Leon's alarm was to divert to himself the blow intended for his friend. For a moment the yellow, devilish face of the boatman bent over him with a look of indescribable malice, the next the axe descended full on poor De Leon's helpless head, and with a groan he sank unconscious into the bottom of the boat.

The boatman turned in time to see that Montgomery was

awake and feeling for his pistol, then, recognizing that the game was up, he jumped ashore.

When he got to the distance of about a hundred yards from the boat, and so out of pistol range, he raised his rifle, which he had taken up as he left the boat, and fired. Thanks, however, to poor De Leon's thoughtfulness in saturating the ruffian's cartridges, the latter's murderous intentions were foiled although he tried shell after shell before he gave up as useless his efforts to kill Montgomery.

The latter, oblivious of the murderer's persistent attempts to shoot him, was stooping over his wounded friend endeavoring to stay the frightful loss of blood from the blow given him by the native. The wound had not been what it had been intended to be —immediately fatal. When De Leon saw the axe descending he had moved his head so as to evade the full force of the weapon which had accordingly somewhat glanced in its stroke.

Still the wound, although not instantly fatal, bid fair to prove so ere long, and Montgomery groaned when he thought of his inability to render his friend skilled assistance.

When he saw that the hemorrhage still continued in spite of all his efforts, a feeling of desperate helplessness seized upon him and his eyes scanned the land to see whether any possible help was within sight.

While his glance was turned towards the prairie a boat suddenly collided gently with his own, and, to his amazement, he found a powerful Indian seated in a birch canoe alongside.

The Indian made a cordial yet dignified signal of friendship, and almost exhausted his English vocabulary with his greeting, "How do?"

In despair, the other pointed to his dying companion and then to the woods beyond, indicating that the murderer had fled.

The Indian took in the situation at a glance, and paddling to the shore he gathered from the armless socket of an aged live oak, a handful of spiders' webs; this done, he removed the other bandages and placed the webs against the wound.

The fine clinging meshes of the webs did what the cloths had failed to do, and the terrible bleeding stopped. De Leon opened his eyes at length, and his friend rejoiced to see that he was sensible and as yet, at least, free from fever.

"Friend, come here to me," faintly whispered the wounded man, after looking wistfully at George Montgomery for a time.

"I am going to leave you, George," and his voice rested tenderly as a woman's on the other's name; "and now that I am dying I want to tell you about a wrong I did you. Stoop lower."

CHAPTER IX.

ALICE MONTGOMERY'S health steadily drooped as the weeks went by and brought no sign from her husband in reply to her loving message, and when at length she received the letter written by her husband on leaving the monastery its utter hopelessness served only to add to her misery and to further undermine her health.

"We must take our poor darling south for the winter," said the old grandmother to her husband, "or we shall lose her," and her sad-eyed partner sighed acquiescence.

For Alice, the spring of her life seemed broken, and look which way she would, the horizon seemed dark and hopeless.

Her brother's malady showed no signs of improvement; he went about pursued by a thousand phantasmal monetary cares—a craze of his brain for which no remedy could be provided, and which was only kept within bounds by his habit of spending long hours daily in signing imaginary checks in payment of inextinguishable loans.

In the late autumn an incident happened to him which accomplished what his medical advisers had considered to be well-nigh impossible in the ordinary course of nature.

While hanging a picture for his sister one day, the step-ladder on which he stood gave way, and precipitated him through a large pane of thick plate-glass. The sharp edges of the glass cut his face and neck severely and the result was a most terrible and alarming hemorrhage, which was only stopped after such a loss of blood as imperiled for a time the sufferer's life.

This loss, however, served to ease and finally to entirely remove the pressure upon his brain resulting from his bullet wound, and when he came back to consciousness from the long fainting spells which succeeded the loss of blood, he inquired feebly of his sister, where he was, and whether she knew who the man was who had shot him.

His life, from the moment George Montgomery's bullet

had struck him until now, was a complete blank.

When Alice Montgomery learned from her brother's lips what had taken place between him and her husband on the night of the quarrel, she, gentle soul, had no blame for the latter, although she loaded herself with bitter reproaches.

"My poor husband; what *must* he have thought to see me meeting and kissing another man surreptitiously, when he believed I had no male relative living excepting the one in this house!"

Her husband's letter had prepared her for her brother's confession, but the details, as furnished by the latter, showed that the crime had been the result of but a momentary frenzy of jealousy which, as a woman, she could readily forgive.

When she took her first walk out of doors with her invalid brother, the last shock of autumn had stripped the trees and covered the sward with a dense matting of leaves which the colored gardener was leisurely removing with a large rake.

For a while the two stopped to speak to the old servitor, and then the latter resumed his work.

Suddenly Alice sprang with a cry from her brother's side and seized the gardener's rake.

"Stop! I saw something flash in the light just where your rake is."

Softly she turned over the crumpled mass and there, at last, lying on a withered chestnut leaf, and round and clear as the first day it was made, lay the wedding-ring lost on that fateful morning, so many weary months ago.

Hidden in the dense green of the turf during the summer season, it had become exposed by the withering of the grass, only to be presently covered by the falling leaves.

First glancing at the initials and date cut on the inside of the hoop to see that there was no chance of a mistake, Alice pressed the ring again and again to her lips, cooing and murmuring glad words of love to herself the while.

"This is my wedding-ring," she exclaimed to her greatly astonished brother, "which I lost on the day of your—your first accident, and all my trouble, I am sure, resulted from that loss. Now its recovery seems like an omen of good luck. Oh, I wonder where on the face of the world my dear husband is! I want to send him a message to tell him that all will be right if he will only come back." And then as the apparent hopelessness of his return came back to her mind, the bright light died out of her eyes, and she resumed the walk with her brother in silence.

At the same hour George Montgomery learned for the first time from his dying comrade's lips about the message which his wife had sent him by cable: "Come back; all is well."

He had no words of reproach for the man who had atoned for the harm which he had done by sacrificing his life for him, but even in the midst of his great and new-found happiness, he groaned to think what dire complications the want of a reply to that message might have entailed.

The Indian had towed the boat to the shores of the beautiful Lake Rosalie, in whose wonderful hammocks that branch of the Seminole tribe which still clung to the Grand Mico, Tallahassee, had long built their wigwams.

The Indians bore the wounded man gently up the bluff on a deer-skin litter, and laid him on a soft couch of prepared Spanish moss, or old man's beard, as it is sometimes called.

Over the sick man's couch a great live oak flung its protecting shade, high above and impermeable to either sun or rain. On all sides the same gigantic trees with their dense evergreen foliage, towered to the skies, their vast limbs festooned with the long draperies of the flowing Spanish moss. A wide open space lay within a vast forest of these trees. The space was large enough for the encampment of an army, and as the mighty span of the live oak branches enabled them to overlap far overhead, the whole looked like some vast cathedral ornamented with delicate fretwork and bathed in a soft and appropriate religious gloom.

To the left of the wounded man lay beautiful Lake Rosalie, across whose broad bosom a refreshing breeze swept which fanned his fevered brow.

To his right, and far within the natural retreat, stood a cluster of wigwams, in whose entrances could be seen groups of squaws of all ages curiously regarding the new arrivals.

After a proper interval had elapsed, the aged Chief Tallahassee, came forward from his tent to greet George Montgomery. The chief was a man of commanding and exceedingly dignified appearance. He was evidently in nowise forgetful of the glories of the tribe of which he was head, even although that tribe should have dwindled down to a mere handful.

The braves who stood by his side were men of gigantic stature, and the Czar of all the Russias owns not warrior more true, or courtiers more obedient or of superior address.

The turbaned heads, clear aquiline features, and long wavy hair served to distinguish this race from all others on the continent of America. Beside their intellectual faces and stalwart frames, the cunning and ferocious Apache, with his meaner physique, shifty eye and animal profile, looked as the hyena looks beside the royal-looking lion.

George Montgomery despatched a letter to his wife, availing himself of the services of an Indian to reach the nearest postal point.

Allowing an interval of ten days to elapse, the same Indian returned by his direction for a reply.

None, however, came either that week or the next, and after the third week the Indian went back no more, and the gloom returned to George Montgomery's brow.

He would fain have sped northward himself to investigate the cause of this silence, but his dying friend still lingered, and as his end drew near he seemed more eagerly to crave the other's society.

"George—it will not be long—wait and close my eyes, and say a Christian prayer over my grave."

And George, in sore trouble, waited.

At length it was clear that the end was at hand and poor De Leon begged his friend not to leave his side that day. As George sat by the other's couch his ear caught now and then the utterances of delirium of his dying comrade.

"George! they are coming, and will soon be here. If they come before the sun sinks behind Lake Rosalie, I shall die happy."

Then he slumbered, and George's head sank on his breast in sad and heavy meditation.

"See! they are coming!" suddenly cried De Leon, rousing from his stupor and startling the various members of the tribe within sound.

George glanced anxiously at his friend, who was now struggling to a sitting position, and pointing across the lake.

"Look! look!" continued the dying man, "they have come in time."

As Montgomery's eyes followed the other's hand, he saw, far in the distance, a small steam-boat crossing the lake. He leaped to his feet and then sat down, bitterly adding aloud, "Why should I excite myself, it is probably a party of surveyors."

An hour later, George Montgomery and Alice, his wife, stood hand in hand by the death-bed of De Leon, and the latter's dying eyes seemed only to have waited for this, for when they saw the happy reunion, they smiled a last benediction and then closed forever.

The meeting between husband and wife, inexpressible as it was in words, was a profound surprise to both. Mrs. Montgomery had gone South at her grandmother's request, and George's first letter was still following her. During their stay in Florida the old lady heard that Chief Tallahassee was camped near Lake Rosalie, and she conceived the brilliant idea of visiting her former friend, and, at the same time, lending some additional interest to her grand-daughter's life.

With some difficulty she had secured the use of a small steam-yacht, with what result the reader already knows.

Tallahassee and two of his braves were absent when the boat arrived.

When the former silently entered the camp, rifle in hand, he found himself suddenly face to face with Mrs. Montgomery and the elder lady.

As he saw Alice, a wonderful light leapt to his eyes, and in the soft Seminole tongue he murmured: "It is the Water-Lily come back," and he stooped and kissed the fair young hand which hung by her side.

"Ah, no, Tallahassee," exclaimed the elder lady, with a rising mist in her eyes and a quiver in her voice which showed that she forgave the present neglect for the sake of the old and faithful memory, "Water-lilies fade as even great warriors fade. I am the friend whose husband you saved at Homosassa, and this new Water-Lily is my grand-daughter."

Tallahassee recognized his error, and his eyes had a soft and tender light in them, as he scanned the aged though still beautiful lineaments of the woman he had known and loved so many years ago. Then he gently took her hand and raised it to his lips, saying tenderly as he did so, "The Water-Lily blooms afresh every spring, but Tallahassee, the Seminole, fades and dies."

That night, as the full-orbed moon shone on the waters of Lake Rosalie, Alice explained fully what had only been whispered when they met. Her brother, she told her husband, had recovered, and no one save themselves knew who had wounded him. He, on his part, explained that some one else had received the message she had sent to Madrid begging him to return; but the name of the man who had received it, he did not divulge, so that in mingling her tears with those of her husband over De Leon's lonely grave by Lake Rosalie, there was no bitterness from the thought of wrong done by the dead.

As George replaced on his wife's hand the ring which had been lost, their eyes met in a long eloquent glance, misty with happy tears. "I will take good care not to take it off again, darling,—that is what you mean, is it not?—for I am sure that whatever others may say, *we* will always believe that it is very unlucky either to take off or lose one's wedding-ring."

THE
LEGEND OF THE RED MOSS RAPIDS.

"IS this the spot where the knight of the old legend was killed, Rowell?"

"Yes, dear, he died on these sharp, spear-pointed rocks, and the old folks living around here who remember the particulars as they were handed down through long generations, say that the rocks assumed that shape and the moss for the first time put on that peculiar blood tint after the murder. Imagination, no doubt; still the combination is certainly a very weird one."

"Suppose you tell me the legend, dear, while we sit on this sloping bank; but, first of all, let me ask, was not the knight who was killed an ancestor of yours?"

"Our family is descended from his brother, Sir Gawain Erfert, whose likeness you saw in the picture gallery."

"What! that strange, stern-looking knight in mail with his hand resting on the cross handle of his sword?"

"Yes, dear, he was the real founder of our family."

"And now for the legend, dear," said the fair Hilda, a beautiful girl of nineteen with large, dark, sympathetic eyes, and a smile whose brightness lit up all the shaded landscape.

Still, Rowell hesitated, and his naturally serious, almost sombre, air, took on more than a touch of gloom.

The two were betrothed lovers, and their wedding was fixed for the following June. Their engagement had suffered from none of the vicissitudes which are supposed to imperil the course of true love. This was largely owing to the depth of their mutual attachment, but it was also due in no small degree to the perfect compatibility of their natures. She was all sweetness and gentleness; he all calmness and strength, with apparently none of the usual masculine waywardness which is more prone to cloud than to illuminate the lover's horizon.

"I am waiting, sir," expostulated the gentle Hilda, nestling much closer to his side than was necessary to a successful hearing.

"Do you really want to hear that unhappy legend, dear?" replied Rowell. "It is a miserable story, and the consequences of what took place here so long ago have left a poison in our family tree which has showed itself in every generation since, in some painful way. Ever since that time, when the Knight Templar died on these rocks, five hundred years ago, some wretched blunder, like an echo of the old one, has occurred time and again to cloud each generation with misery and self-reproach; and caused the family to be known throughout the whole North Country as the "Gloomy Erferts." When I tell you the story, which is shown by the old chronicles to be a dismally true one in every detail, and in that respect different from many other Border Legends, you may, perhaps, not care to become a member of such an ill-starred house. The risk, dear, seems to me to be quite considerable," and the smile with which Rowell looked into the eyes of his *fiancée* had infinitely more of wistfulness and pathos in it than was good to see in one so young.

"Oh, Rowell, do you think me a child! Our marriage is now so near that I consider myself one of the family already; and you would not hide my own family's secrets from me would you?"

To Rowell, the warm pressure of the locked hands, the arch, lovelit glance, and the magnetism of the beautiful girl-woman at his side were irresistible; and taking the dainty head between his hands he kissed the upturned face again and again—eyes, hair, lips—in a burst of passion which left the fair Hilda's cheeks all aglow, and her eyes eloquent with a struggle between rebellion and rapture.

"Now, to business, sir, if you have got over your outbreak of lunacy," resumed the still blushing Hilda, as she regained possession of herself, and moved, with much pretence of distance, a foot away.

Rowell, seeing there was no escape, took up the recital of the legend, but there was a protest in his tones, which roused a look of remonstrance in his listener.

"When the second Crusade failed," began Rowell, "among the surviving English knights who drifted slowly back to their homes, across Europe, enfeebled by wounds and the pestilential climate in which they had endured such untold hardships in their efforts to rescue the Holy City from the Infidel, there was a Knight Templar who for special valor in rescuing the person of the Preceptor as well as the sacred standard of his Order after their capture by the Saracens, was, at his request, absolved from his vows of celibacy by the Grand Master.

"This meant a retirement from the sacred Order, and as the latter's rules recognized no form of withdrawal, or absolution from its vows save by death, the elaborate ceremonial customary on the death of a great knight was observed and the Knight Templar obtained his freedom only after the due performance of his funeral obsequies. The fame and position of these knights and of their spiritual order was so great that it is difficult to imagine any knight craving release.

"The explanation of the strange request, however, was to be found in the fact that this knight, after taking his vows, had met and had fallen hopelessly in love with a beautiful woman, the Lady Erminie Athelrade, and the love was fully reciprocated.

"A mutual confession of attachment had taken place, and the knight left with the apparently hopeless task before him of earning absolution from his vows by some unparalleled service to the Order. Failing success—and fulfilment of their desires had seemed beyond earthly possibilities—their only hope lay in some future reward for their constancy, beyond the grave, for the knight was of stainless character and would rather have suffered death a thousand times at the hands of the Paynim hosts than have betrayed his vows. So the knight had left England for the Holy Land, breathing the sentiment which found voice hundreds of years later: 'I could not love thee, dear, so much, loved I not honor more.'

"You will now understand with what feelings the knight —now no longer a Templar, but simply Sir Julian Erfert—found himself, wounded and war-beaten, it is true, but still alive, back in his native country; in the same little island as the woman he worshipped, whose image, glowing in his heart like a holy flame, had inspired him to deeds which had thrilled Christendom and beggared all knightly possibilities.

"Sir Julian, I ought to say, had one confidant of his passion, his elder brother, Sir Rowell.

"When Sir Julian arrived in England, no one would have recognized in the battered knight, innocent of followers, the former princely Templar, whose splendor of apparel and of retinue had elicited so much applause when he left to join the Crusaders five years before.

"It was late one summer afternoon, in early June, when Sir Julian rode up to the Castle of Barronby, where he had left the Lady Erminie in the care of her guardian, the Earl of Wolston, a man, the knight now recollected with a chill of apprehension, notorious for his grasping and ambitious nature.

"Sir Julian had had no tidings of the lady since he had left, and he had sent her no love message, ever mindful of the fact that it would be death to the fair reputation of any dame to have her name breathed by a Templar, or to have it known that she was interested in his welfare. He had sent her word of the accomplishment of his release, but whether or not his message had perished by the way in those perilous times he could not tell. He had forwarded a letter to his brother, too, and so there he was at last under the shadow of Castle Barronby's walls, with his heart throbbing as it had never beat even when a dozen Saracen blades were at his throat and the gleam of his Red Cross banner was lost among the tossing crescents of the Infidel host.

"As he gathered rein for an instant in an open glade, a foot soldier, unarmed and with his head-casque gone, tottered into the opening and fell with a moan into the heavy grass. On seeing this strange sight, the knight dismounted and stooped over the soldier, who was evidently badly wounded.

"After he had unlaced the fainting man's jerkin the soldier opened his eyes, and seeing Sir Julian, strove to rise, while his hollow voice struggled for utterance.

" 'Sir Knight, go tell the Earl, the Lady Athelrade has been carried off and her guard killed.'

" 'How many, and which way did they go?' briefly inquired the knight.

" 'Full half a score spearmen and a knight whose crest I could not see. They went by Swivel's Moss, on the Umber Road,' and he said no more but fell back dead.

"The knight gave no glance to the castle, but he looked to his saddle girths, untied the mace at his saddle-bow, loosened the heavy sword in its sheath, and swung into the saddle humming softly a quaint eastern air which made his gallant charger crane back his ears to hear, and took all the fatigue out of his weary limbs. 'This is like the old times, Salado,' said the knight softly to his Arab, and the horse leapt at the words.

"The knight looked young again. 'This is as my soul desired to win her, at the sword's point. Heaven is good. And here is Swivel's Moss, and there lies the Umber Road. Now, Salado!'

"Half an hour more and the Mivern Rapids could be heard. A few minutes later and the glint of helmets came to the rider through the trees. 'We shall catch them at the ford, Salado,' and the words gave new life to the willing Arab, who came of a fighting race, and to whom fighting was the very breath of life. 'Ten to one, Salado, dare we venture?' and the knight laughed softly to himself, and the flying steed shook his sides as if he too chuckled at the thought.

"A minute more, and the knight found himself face to face with the abductors, who, hearing pursuit, had gathered themselves into line on the edge of the ford.

"Yes, there they were, fully half a score and a knight with visor down, and without a crest, in command, and on the further side a female figure on horseback being hurried on in advance, on either side of her a well-armed soldier.

" 'Surrender the lady,' shouted the knight through the bars of his visor.

" 'To whom?' came back the haughty inquiry.

" 'To her friend and Earl Wolston.'

"The strange knight laughed.

" 'Tell the Earl,' he said, 'the lady is a willing fugitive, and will not return.'

"Sir Julian made no response, but Salado felt the touch— no more—of a gilded spur and shot forward like an arrow from a bow. The men-at-arms were stout and willing, but three of them fell from their seats like dummies before the whirl of that demoniac mace; and the gallant Arab fought no less willingly and mangled the opposing steeds. The odds were terrible, but such odds were familiar, and the solitary warrior was not without his chances. He had almost cleared a path, and even in the frenzy of fight his brain was troubled to know why the lady made no sign. Another horseman overthrown, and he stood face to face with the leader, exchanged with him ringing blows, which could be heard far above the roar of the rapids, on whose edge they fought. Once more the spur touched Salado, and the mace beat down the leader's guard. Victory was in sight, almost, when, alas! the gallant Arab's foot sank in the ooze of the river, and his suddenly arrested movement threw horse and rider into the shallow torrent. Sir Julian struggled to extricate himself and to rise to his feet, but half a dozen spears hemmed him in and drank his blood through the rifts in his armor made by the pointed rocks. The struggle of his horse carried him beneath the current, the surging flood filled his closed casque, and a long and last good-night fell, in his native land, on the knight who had survived all the dangers of the terrible Crusade. No, at least not yet, the leader knight, now unhelmeted, directed his spearmen to raise the dying knight and carry him to shore. But a javelin of rock between his shoulder-plates held him fast while he was bleeding to death from spear thrusts.

"When his helmet was unbarred he regained the consciousness temporarily lost, and his dying eyes wandered from the faces of the men around him to that of their leader. The sight of the latter seemed to trouble him, and he strove feebly to clear his eyes from the spray of the water and the mist of approaching death. 'My brother, can it be?' he murmured hoarsely.

"But why prolong the dismal story. It was his brother, Sir Rowell, who had carried out the abduction of the lady. He had heard that the Earl was about to wed the Lady Erminie to his nephew for the sake of her lands, and having received his brother's message from the Holy Land and communicated its contents to the lady, an abduction was arranged as the only possible means of preventing a forced marriage. He had intended that his wife, the Lady Rowell, should give safe sanctuary to Erminie until Julian returned, when the two long-parted lovers should be united.

"The knight died in the arms of the lady he loved. Her lips consoled him—dying—for life's disappointment. 'Wait for me,' were the last words he heard on earth, and his waiting was short, for as his eyes closed in death she drew the dagger from his belt and with it liberated her own soul, so that it could—not follow—but accompany him. They were buried together, and they left behind them the saddest man in all the world, my ancestor, Sir Rowell, whose terrible share in that fatal mistake—

innocent enough in all conscience—has left all his descendants a heritage of penance, showing that Nature, like man, never forgets or forgives a blunder, or rather that she fails to discriminate between a crime and a blunder, and punishes or rewards only according to results.

"The tragedy of the rapids has been repeated in our family time and again down through the intervening centuries, not as tragedies perhaps, but as unhappy blunders—echo-like repetition of the first—such as have worked untold miseries to all the race.

"Now, darling, that I have told you the true legend of the Red Moss Rapids, do you still wish to marry into so dismal a family?"

"Yes, yes, more than ever; before it was simply a pleasure, now it is also a duty."

"In what way, dearest?"

"Ah, that is my secret, sir, only to be revealed on our wedding day; but, tell me, was there no sequel to that terrible tragedy?"

"Well, my ancestor, who was the innocent cause of the slaying of Sir Julian, said on his death-bed that in the far distance he foresaw a time when the shadow consequent on his fatal error would be lifted from our house, but it would only happen when some descendant of the Athelrade family, who should be ignorant of all the circumstances, had of her own free will revived the traditions of the celebrated Order of the Templars.

"It was thought that grief had to some extent crazed the old knight's brain, and that in the long trances which he was subject to prior to his death his burning desire to right the wrong he had inadvertently done—which had grown to be a perfect monomania with him—had put strange fancies into his head, and that as he imagined the misfortune which fell on our house had come through the slight done to the Order of the Templars by his brother's retirement from it, even under proper dispensation, he grew in time to believe that peace could only come to the house again through some member of the Athelrade family (Lady Athelrade being the person who, so to speak, tempted Sir Julian) doing what I have stated."

"Dear me," remarked the fair Hilda, "how those fine old knights used to worry about things; just fancy any soldier of the present day distressing himself on his death-bed about an unlucky accident for which he was in no way to blame, and torturing his last moments with the forecast of what was going to happen three hundred years later."

"Yes, it does seem strange," returned her companion, "that these knights who seemed in many respects so much more cruel and bloodthirsty than men of the present day, should yet have had worries and anxieties which even the most delicate and nervous lady of the nineteenth century would despise. They were a strange medley, those knights of old, steeping Europe in blood for a mere idea, and dying cheerfully themselves if in their final departure they could but kiss a lock of some fair creature some thousands of miles away, whom they adored. Oh, enthusiasm is a great, an immeasurably great force. Tallyrand says: 'Point de zèle—point de zèle,' but his clarion-trumpeted cry of 'No zeal, no zeal,' is a vast mistake I think.

"His maxim may be all right for statesmen and diplomatists, but when the zealot dies from off the earth, one of Nature's grandest forces will disappear."

"Thank you, dear, that was quite an interesting little homily," archly ventured Hilda, as she wooed her lover back to present and more attractive pursuits by placing her lovely arms round his neck. "Now, suppose you tell me, my hero, what you will give me if I can erase all that dark inky stain from your family escutcheon, in addition to providing you with a brand-new bride?"

"Well, cara-mia, I am afraid it is not to be done; what you

term the ink stain has been there too long. My little sweetheart, who cannot find acidity enough for her daily life, and is imposed upon all the time on that account, certainly cannot evolve any acid strong enough to clear away a stain which has grown deeper with the centuries. No, dearest, if you insist upon marrying me after my recent disclosure, I am afraid you will find that the ill-fate will follow us, and that our union will be indeed for woe as well for weal."

"Fie upon you, sir, for such gloomy thoughts; they are unworthy of my future husband, and I protest against them. Yes, sir,—in this way," and her rosy lips stole upwards to his after a fashion that effectually erased everything but Paradise from his mind.

The wedding-day must have been Hymen's own selection. The morning broke bright and clear with that dewy freshness in the air only to be found in Merrie England.

"Happy the bride the sun shines on," a hundred pair of loving lips murmured in joyous congratulation to the dainty white-robed figure crowned with orange blossoms.

Surely never since time began did wedding-bells sound so merrily and so sweetly on the palpitating air as on that morning when the proud and happy Rowell led the fair Hilda from the altar. Forgotten were all ill-fated ancestry and gloomy legends. The past rolled itself up hastily and convulsively, as a roll of long-kept musty vellum bounds back into its old-time shape, and only the happy, glorious, untranslateable present remained. Words of gracious congratulation fell in showers on the ears of the blissful pair as sweet June flowers fell beneath their feet; but they scarcely heard or saw, so much greater was the joyous tumult in their happy blissful hearts.

. . . .

"Hilda, my darling," inquired the happy husband when his breath had come back to him, and they were seated behind a pair of high-stepping horses on their way to the railway station, with suspicious traces of rice still visible on their travelling attire, "I noticed you signed your name in the marriage register as Hilda Athelrade Erfert of Temple Newsam!"

"Yes, dearest, and you want to know how I come to use the name of Athelrade? Well, dear, I am a descendant of the Athelrade family. And O, my darling, I must confess something else now—*my secret*. I am also the owner of Temple Newsam—the innocent restorer of the tombs of the Knight Templars, foretold by your ancestor, and O, sweetheart, last and best of all, the destroyer of your family curse, as well as, I hope, the founder of your own particular and individual happiness."

TWO NINETY-DAY OPTIONS.

"IT is a most wretched business, and I wish I were well out of it."

As these words fell from the speaker's lips his strong right hand smote the portals in front of him, and Delmonico's heavy glass doors swung violently back in response to the vigor of his touch.

Carried away by the force of his feelings, he swung into the restaurant with the full vigor of his mountain stride, and more as if he were a detective in expectation of surprising a gang of coiners than an innocent visitor in quest of congenial society and wholesome fare.

To speak the truth, Douglas Gaskell, a native of Scotland, and mining expert by profession, thought himself in very hard luck indeed this bright summer evening. Not even the hum of cheerful life around him could overcome his despondency or soften the bitter reflections which gnawed at his heart.

And as he reviewed the situation later on under the soothing influences of his cigar and coffee, he still reassured himself that he had most excellent grounds for repining, if not indeed for despairing altogether.

Glancing backward a few months he saw himself returning to his native land after many long years of self-denial and hardship in the mining districts of India and South Africa, with enfeebled health, a few hundred pounds, a good reputation for honesty in a business of some temptations, and a ripe experience in mining matters.

Then, in his retrospect, amid the hum of cheerful humanity around him, he saw the fairest face in Scotland smiling on him; he saw an obdurate old Scottish laird, who utterly refused to let his daughter be engaged to a "penniless mining fellow;" and after a long siege by soft, persistent womanhood's irresistible arms, he saw the grim old borderer yield so far as to say that if he, Gaskell, could satisfy him, before he started for

Norway in July, that he had means to maintain his daughter suitably, he would then be willing to consider the propriety of an engagement, on the clear, mutual understanding, however, that Gaskell must sheer off for good if he were unable to satisfy the old man within the three months which he allowed him.

This had been a most despairing decision to the mining expert, who termed it the offer of "A ninety-day option on the woman I love, with impossible conditions, and the wreck of two lives as a forfeit." But Madge, the lady of his heart's affections, had declared everything was possible of achievement to true love within three months; and how his stern face softened as he recalled the bright, hopeful loyal look with which she had dispatched him to London to take counsel with her uncle, her dead mother's favorite brother.

He remembered how the uncle had obtained him a commission to examine an American gold mine, as a step towards finding, on his own account, while in the mining districts of the United States, some good property suitable for the British market.

"If you find such a mine," he had said, "I will do my best to place it for you, and you can honestly add $100,000 to its price as discoverer, if it is large enough, and provided the terms on which you obtain the control will justify it. That is the only way that occurs to me in which you can honestly comply with the old curmudgeon's absurd conditions within the time."

The face of the silent and absorbed man grew dark as he recalled how, in the execution of his commission, he had arrived in New York only to learn that the property he came to examine had been withdrawn from the market.

The fact was that the gentleman who had offered the property in London, and who had accompanied him across the ocean to introduce him to the proprietors, had taken his measure accurately during the voyage, and had reported to his colleagues and joint owners that he was quite satisfied that Gaskell could not be tampered with, but would insist upon making a thorough examination, such as must inevitably disclose the worthlessness of the property. The owners were simply a gang of unscrupulous adventurers, who had thought to avail themselves of the existing craze for American mining properties.

It was the announcement of the withdrawal of the property which had plunged Douglas Gaskell into the depths of despondency in which this narrative finds him.

As his retrospection ended he sat lost in thought, and barely conscious of the ebb and flow of the city's gilded youth, and the men of affairs who throng Delmonico's in ever-increasing numbers.

He was all unconsciously being very closely observed by three gentlemen seated at a distant table. Mr. Oswald, who had accompanied him across from England; Hector Marble and Hamilton Gilbey, all "speculators" in other people's money. They were, in fact, the owners of the withdrawn mine. Mr. Gilbey broke the silence at their table. "It is just as easy to make a large haul as a small one," he said. "We must manage to fix something up for this Scotch expert who is sitting over there looking so glum. He is disappointed at our withdrawal of this mine, and is, I imagine, ready for a fresh suggestion. Now I have been casting about for something to suit him, and I think I have discovered it at last."

The three drew their chairs closer together than strictly honest men found it necessary to do in Delmonico's, and the champagne in their glasses grew flat, and their cigars went out, while the one expounded and the two received and approved one of the choicest plans which villainy has ever concocted in connection with international syndicate or corporate business.

The proposition laid by Mr. Gilbey before his colleagues with much graphic force and a wealth of luminous illustration began with the preamble, They must have money. The Scotchman sitting near by suggested a means of getting it; he was only useful in connection with mines; he could not be fooled as to the quality of a mine, therefore he must be fooled in some other way, as they could not promptly get the control of any honest mine on terms which would be acceptable to the syndicate and profitable to them. That was the argument, and it was considered as being to the point. The proposition was as follows: Gilbey knew of a mine called "The Gold Queen" in California, which had at one time embraced a great number of claims and covered quite an extent of territory. This mine became quite a valuable property, and a dispute having arisen as to the ownership of one-half of it, the property was finally divided between the two litigants by decision of the Court of Appeals. Both properties retained the title of "Gold Queen," and openings had been made in both about 700 yards apart. The workings in one mine had proved enormously successful, and that mine could not be purchased. The other had resulted in failure, and very little, if any, labor was now being expended on it.

Mr. Gilbey's suggestion was that the "Gold Queen" mine, which had proved a failure, should be optioned to the English syndicate, and that while its survey should be correctly given on the option, steps should be taken to get Mr. Gaskell to examine the good mine, under the belief that he was inspecting the one optioned to his syndicate. "Although you can't deceive him as to the existence of paying ore in a mine," continued Gilbey, "you can readily confuse him as to the identity of the property he is examining, more especially if he is simply a mineralogist and not a surveyor as well."

"I know the manager of the 'Gold Queen' now in operation—number one let us call it—and I can guarantee that he will see this business through if we divide with him. Number one is well known to be well worth a large sum of money, and it won't do for us to offer the other property at less than half a million. The owner of the latter is willing to give me a four months' option on it at $15,000."

Their plans being matured, the illustrious pair were presently introduced to Mr. Gaskell as the owners of the mine which had been withdrawn. They had exerted themselves, they said, to find him a property of equal promise, and had at last, after much trouble, succeeded in obtaining for him an option on the "Gold Queen."

Mr. Gaskell had notified Madge's uncle of his first disappointment by cable, and two hours after meeting Gilbey's partners he walked across Madison Square and sent another cablegram intimating that he had heard of another property, and was about to go West to examine it at his own expense.

Two days later Mr. Gaskell left for San Francisco, where, on his arrival, he met the manager of the "Gold Queen" No. 1, who had received a telegram from Mr. Gilbey to go to San Francisco to receive an important letter, which letter he had carefully read and very cordially approved.

The days which followed had many anxious moments for the three speculators in New York.

"I do most devoutly hope this business won't land us in State's prison," murmured the less courageous Marble.

"What nonsense. We have not made any incriminating statement in writing."

"True, but you forget your letter to the manager of the mine. Won't that show conspiracy?"

"That is all right," was Gilbey's airy rejoinder; "the manager is under my thumb."

"By the way," continued the tranquil Gilbey, "did you notice that Gaskell had the ninety days' option which you gave him made to himself personally, and not as representing the syndicate?"

"Yes," replied Oswald, "I noticed it. He would not take the responsibility of spending the syndicate's money in making investigations which the members had not ordered. If he approves the property he will recommend it to his syndicate."

A soft, sweet, childlike smile crept over the faces of the precious three as they separated.

A fortnight later Mr. Gilbey presented to his delighted associates the following dispatch from Gaskell, dated San Francisco:

"I approve of the mine optioned, subject to some amendment in price, and start East to-night.

"Douglas Gaskell."

When Mr. Gaskell returned to New York he said he had made a very careful examination of the mine, and would be willing to accept an option for it if the price were fixed at $250,000 instead of double that sum. The radical curtailment of their figures somewhat dampened the ardor of the three confederates, but finally the price was fixed at $325,000 cash, with many protests on the part of Messrs. Marble and Gilbey. Mr. Oswald had throughout taken only such interest in the matter as a friend might manifest. His name did not occur on any of the papers given Mr. Gaskell, and on this occasion as on the others, he took little part in the arrangements.

In due time the purchase money was paid over, and Messrs. Marble & Gilbey, each with $100,000 to his credit, decided that they would seize the opportunity to satisfy a long-felt ambition to explore Southern America, not in the least—they were careful to assure the cynical Oswald—because they were fearful as to what view the cold judicial eye of the law might take of their action in connection with the mine they had sold.

Mr. Oswald, who, as stated, had purposely kept in the background, and in consequence contented himself with a smaller share of the profits, remained in New York.

· · · · · · · · · · ·

Six months later Messrs. Gilbey and Marble were in the city of Mexico, wearied beyond the power of words with the vaunted charms of that country, and anxious only to be once more within sight of New York. Many a time they echoed the sentiment of the city wanderer at which we smile so often, "I would rather be a lamp-post on Broadway than a king anywhere else."

But respite was at hand. A letter to Mr. Oswald, making apparently casual inquiry as to whether he had heard anything further of the "Gold Queen" sale, elicited the following characteristic reply:

"If you are cooping yourselves up in the city of Mexico because you are afraid to return on account of any troublesome developments in the 'Gold Queen' business, you may as well come back at once. The Englishmen have not discovered their blunder, and I do not think they ever will. I have a good story to tell you which is worth your while to come 3,000 miles to hear. Meet me at dinner on the 8th, usual time and place, and I'll tell you the story. There's no place like home!"

Within three hours the two speculators were on the way to New York.

When the second bottle of champagne had been opened at Mr. Oswald's dinner the host lit a cigar, saying he supposed they were dying to hear his story.

The lips of the two twitched a little, and a hardly perceptible pallor indicated a passing nervousness.

"When the Scotchman got to the mine," Oswald began, "the manager took him to 'Gold Queen' No. 1, as you (or as we) arranged. He remained under ground forty-eight hours. The manager was cautioned not to lose sight of him for a moment, but he gave in after thirty-six hours and went home to bed, as the Scot looked like spending a week in the bowels of the earth. When the manager returned, twelve hours later, he found Gaskell just coming to the surface. In reply to his inquiry he said he had completed his investigation and would take some rest. Whether this was merely a blind to put the manager off his guard, or whether he changed his mind, I don't know, but after he had seen the other descend the mine, and had had some breakfast, he took the map which you gave him out of his valise and proceeded very carefully to compare it—first, with the boundaries of the No. 1 mine, which some loafing miner pointed out to him at his request, and then with the map of the same mine hanging in the company's office, and which the manager had stupidly omitted to remove.

"As nearly as can be computed, it took that fellow just about five minutes to detect the trick. Of course this is mere guess-work, for the man himself was as silent as a clam. The profundity of his silence when he unravelled our tangled plots aroused my admiration.

"After he learned the game, he placidly descended Mine No. 2, the one of which he really held the option. He remained in that mine just sixteen hours, and all that time the manager concluded he was in bed and asleep. I'm sure I don't know why, except on the assumption that a man must sleep sometime.

"With the assistance of an old Mexican miner, who practically lives down in that mine, in one of the shafts, he thoroughly explored the mine, more especially at that part which is in a straight line with the rich vein of No. 1.

"He had to all appearances some queer theory about that vein, for he and the old Mexican worked for more than twelve hours cutting in its direction. The result of these efforts was (it was ascertained after the purchase) that while the Mexican slept Gaskell struck a continuation of the vein belonging to No. 1. Having satisfied himself that he had struck the true vein and after taking out several specimens of the ore, he carefully covered up his 'find,' awoke the old man and returned to the surface.

"You will understand the discovery Gaskell had made when I tell you that from the vein in No. 1 to where it was identified in No. 2 is just 700 yards, of which 550 run through the land of No. 2, so that 11.14 of the great vein belong to the mine that Gaskell bought.

"Well, gentlemen, Gaskell sold that mine to his syndicate —it was his own venture—for $750,000, half cash, half stock, and his syndicate sold it to the public for $1,500,000. The new company has already taken $500,000 out of the mine in four months' working, with the prospect of taking out twenty times as much in the next two years. The Scotsman's profit of $325,000 taken in stock is now worth $1,000,000 in the market."

Marble and his associates gazed at each other fixedly for a minute, and although their eyes spoke volumes, no word was uttered. The situation was altogether too deep for words. With one impulse they rose in grim silence from the table. "I find the air in this room suffocating," finally ejaculated Gilbey, "let us go."

As the now silent trio passed into the vestibule in making their exit to Fifth Avenue, Oswald shattered his preternatural calm by ejaculating: "Great Jupiter!" The exclamation was not surprising, for there, coming toward them, was Mr. Gaskell, the man they had done their best to swindle, and his bride, the beautiful and queenly Madge. For a moment a wavering in the ranks of the three was perceptible, and just the suspicion of a desire to stampede, but the expression on the expert's face reassured them.

"My dear," he said, addressing his wife, "let me present to you some friends of mine who once rendered me a very great service—somewhat inadvertently it is true"—(a faint shiver shook the three)—"but nevertheless a genuine service. They helped me to win what I wanted most on earth," and his eyes rested fondly on his wife.

Mrs. Gaskell commented to her husband afterward on the strange, shy modesty which almost prevented the three gentlemen from meeting her gaze, and his smiling reply was,

"They couldn't stand the battery, dear."

After the three friends had escaped into the street from the (to them) terrible situation, Oswald, probably for the first time in his life, wore a crestfallen air. "Boys," he said, "he carries too many guns for us all round. Just think of it, he has never even mentioned to her the—to put it mildly—somewhat peculiar part we took in the mining deal."

"How do you know that?"

"Because you can always tell by the expression in a woman's eyes, when you are presented to her, how her husband has been in the habit of speaking about you to her. I would rather have faced a hair-trigger revolver than those great gray eyes if she had known our game."

Mr. Gaskell has taken other ninety-day options since his marriage, and some of them have proved very valuable, but he never expects to find one to equal that marvellous pair by which he won both fortune and bride in 1888.

MR. JOHNSTONE'S INFIRMITY.

"Felix Johnstone! What a name, mamma! There is a great want of tone about it. Don't you think so? I'm sure I hope the man is presentable, but you know how careless and unobservant Dick is."

The speaker, Maud Ponsonby-Fitzwaring, a lovely girl of some twenty summers, sat, pen in hand, and with her pretty brows all a-pucker, in her mamma's boudoir, scanning the list of names of intended guests of Ormsby Hall during the ensuing shooting season.

"My dear," replied her stately and abundant mamma in a tone which settled the matter, "he is as rich as Crœsus, and even if he should prove eccentric, why he is an Australian, and you know everything is excused in a 'Colonial;' especially," resumed the dame after a brief pause and with more than her usual drawl — "especially if he is very wealthy."

Maud was too young for an argument of this kind to have any weight with her, but she only shrugged her well-poised shoulders by way of protest, and presently the letter of invitation for the Twelfth of August, when grouse shooting commenced, was on its way to Mr. Felix Johnstone.

The person whose name set the dainty Maud's teeth on edge was a stoutly-built, well-preserved gentleman of some forty years, the greater part of whose life had been spent at the Antipodes, where, if he had not acquired much of the polish demanded by polite society, he had, nevertheless, secured a goodly supply of that excellent substitute for it — gold.

When Mr. Felix Johnstone reached the Hall, in response to the invitation, he found that the bulk of the other visitors had already arrived, and to a great extent "sorted" themselves, as he termed it; that is to say, that the males and females had, for the most part, settled upon their friendships for the period of their stay at Ormsby Hall.

This arrangement left the late arrival somewhat out in the cold. It is true that his friend Dick did his best to make him feel at home, but, as the old Squire, Colonel Ponsonby-Fitzwaring, was somewhat gouty, most of his duties as host devolved upon his son, who had in consequence but little time to devote to any particular guest.

"Jarvis," said Mr. Johnstone to his valet the morning after his arrival, "you'll have to keep me posted in things. You know that's what you're here for. Captain Fitzwaring recommended you as being the best man he knew, and Dick—I mean the Captain—knows a good man, if anybody does."

"Yes, sir," responded Jarvis with more of embarrassment than his usually immovable face was wont to show.

"What shall you wear this morning, sir?" inquired the valet, as if anxious to turn the conversation.

"Well, I thought a frock coat and that pair of lavender trousers, which Poole sent in before I left London, and a white waistcoat, would about suit this kind of weather and the style of society hereabouts—these and—of course patent leather shoes."

It could hardly have happened in so well-trained a servant, and yet surely it was the ghost of a smile which his master saw flitting across Jarvis' face.

"Eh! What is it, Jarvis?" inquired Mr. Johnstone sharply, "wont these do?"

"Well, sir," replied the valet with much deference, "most gentlemen wear knickerbockers and lacing boots in the morning when they are going shooting. I thought, perhaps, this velvet jacket and these corduroy trousers, and woollen stockings or gaiters—"

"What, these great coarse things? Why, I was better dressed than that in the 'Bush!'—still," noticing a certain relentlessness of aspect creeping over the well-trained servant's face, "if I must, I must; only it seems to me that there's a great fondness here for showing one's legs. I'm sure the way these flunkies aired their white silk stockings and great calves last night before the ladies was hardly decent. By the way, Jarvis, do you know any of the gentlemen staying here? If you do, just fire away and tell me all about them while I'm dressing myself like a —like a navvy!"

"Well, sir, there's Mr. Granby just walking across the lawn. He is a celebrated barrister, made his reputation as a junior counsel in the Tichborne case; he is likely to get a judgeship out in Bombay soon, they say. The gentleman with him is Mr. Softleigh, editor of the Morning Whisper, a very fashionable paper. That dark-browed swarthy man with the piercing eyes, just lighting his cigar, is Hugo Swinton, the African traveler who had the terrible fight with the great gorilla now in the Zoo. The man waiting for him is Captain Bottomly, of the Guards, who reformed the British square when the Soudanese broke it at—somewhere in Egypt. They say he has six spear wounds in his body."

"But, I say, Lord! Who is that pompous individual dressed in black—the one with the clean shaven face and port-winey complexion?"

"That, sir, is the Bishop of Oldchester," replied Jarvis, with a touch of remonstrance in his tone.

"Well; and even he puts his chubby old calves on exhibition. Is he going shooting too?"

"No, sir," replied Jarvis, with quite an air, as if there were limits to this kind of thing. "All the Bishops wear black tight fitting cloth gaiters; it is their Episcopal dress."

"O, I see; well now, who is that very elegant young gentleman with the cane, bowing to the ladies in the pony carriage?"

"That is a Mr. Elphinstone Howard. I have never seen him before, but they tell me he belongs to one of the County families in the North somewhere. He is not very well acquainted with the gentry around here yet, as he has been brought up abroad where his father was retrenching. He saved Colonel Fitzwaring's life in Florence by stopping a run-away horse, and with that introduction the family took him up and introduced him to English society."

"Well, Jarvis, all of these men seem to be celebrated for something excepting myself. Can you tell me how such a common-place person as I am comes to be here?"

Jarvis did not like to tell Mr. Johnstone that his great wealth was his recommendation, so he evaded the question by inquiring which of his guns he would use that day.

"Oh, bother the guns," was the response, "I don't want to kill anything this beautiful morning. Here, Jarvis, quick!" he called suddenly from the window, "who is that lady driving the ponies?"

"That, sir, is the Lady Evelyn Beeton, daughter of the late Earl of Kingswood."

"Is she very poor, Jarvis?" inquired Mr. Johnstone, after a substantial sigh indicative of dampened hopes at hearing the lady's title.

"No, sir, she is reported to be quite wealthy, as she succeeded to the old Earl's property, excepting the estates which, being entailed in the male line, passed to his nephew."

"I'm sorry to hear it, Jarvis, deuced sorry, for that is the only woman I could ever have loved. Funny thing to tell you, isn't it, but then you are in a way my confidential adviser in this strange, God-forsaken country, and I know you would never split on me, for if you did, Jarvis, I would break your blessed neck to a certainty."

"Yes, sir," replied the complaisant Jarvis, by way of acknowledging the other's kind intentions.

"No, sir," resumed Mr. Felix Johnstone with a burst of enthusiasm, "I'm not one of these men who have all their life long been trailing their hearts through the streets and highways for every thoughtless miss to trample on; my heart is a virgin field to be harvested only by one woman in this world, and if she won't have it so, then, Jarvis, the grain has got to rot on the ground, that's all. Now, Jarvis, there is something about the lady's voice and look which stirs me like a trumpet. I sat opposite her at dinner last night, and the mistakes I made in consequence are something awful to contemplate. You see, Jarvis, she is not too young. She is, I imagine, about thirty——"

"She is thirty-two, sir," respectfully corrected Jarvis, closing a Burke's Peerage at which he had been glancing.

"Well, now, it strikes me, my friend," retorted his master, with a flush on his brow, "that you are infernally precise about the Lady Evelyn Beeton's age. May I take the liberty of inquiring, sir, how you came to know it exactly—just to a hair, as it were?"

There was fire in the master's eye, but the well-trained valet answered with stoical calm. "Her ladyship's age is in the Peerage; sir, I thought it might interest you to know."

The answer was mollifying, but the little outburst called for a lull in the conversation, and Mr. Johnstone, now fully dressed, stood in silence looking out at the window, while the valet busied himself about his master's effects with unruffled brow.

"She has such a high-bred and refined air, and such a soft and musical voice, and her eyes, what wonderful color and expression! And then the figure, so graceful, and yet so rounded. She ought to be a queen, and there I'm only a common Australian squatter and digger."

Such was the murmuring monotone which rolled musically from the massive throat of Felix Johnstone by the window.

"Well—I'm—consumed," he suddenly shouted, "if that jackanapes Howard hasn't got into the pony chaise beside her!

My hat, Jarvis, quick!"

But soon he reined his fury's pace. "After all, it is no business of mine," he resumed, "besides, what could an uncultivated clod like me have in common with a noble refined lady like that! Now if she were only poor or in need of a friend, and," warming to his work, "in danger of her life, there would be some show for me, but as it is, my case is simply hopeless," with which moody reflections Mr. Johnstone slowly wended his way downstairs to a late breakfast.

He found Miss Maud, the daughter of the house, presiding at the breakfast table, with that radiant look and well groomed air peculiar to English country girls, and by and by, when they were left alone, he managed to turn the conversation to the object of his adoration.

"We think all the world of her," remarked his companion. "She is one of nature's true noble-women. She gave up the best years of her life to her invalid father, and now I suppose she will never marry."

"Why it seems to me," quickly replied Johnstone, "that young fellow Howard is paying her marked attention. And he is quite young and very good-looking."

This sentence bore so dismal a tone that Miss Maud looked up, and after regarding the speaker with a demure glance, she arose from the table simultaneously with her *vis-à-vis*, and thereby terminated the morning meal.

As she saw Mr. Johnstone standing on the steps a few minutes later, in a listless attitude uncommon in so stalwart and well-knit a figure, she remarked to herself, "and so you are caught, my handsome but unsophisticated Antipodian."

That evening at dinner an accident occurred which, for a time, assumed the dimensions of a calamity. Colonel Ponsonby-Fitzwaring, it must be stated, was lord lieutenant of the county in which he lived, and although he bore no title he occupied a position and lived in a style unsurpassed by any titled magnate within a hundred miles. Dinners at the Hall under his *régime* assumed the importance of State festivals, and the order of procedence was as carefully observed as at any court ceremony.

At eight o'clock, when the dining-room's stately doors were thrown wide open, it was accordingly a brilliant procession which Colonel Fitzwaring—albeit still somewhat shaky from the gout—headed with the worthy Bishop's lady on his arm. Mrs. Penelope Broadbent was proud of her revered husband, and she was, subject to no deductions, proud, also, of herself. She was a lady of magnificent quantities, and if none of her numerous admirers used the word "stately" in describing her, it was probably because her wealth of proportion was other than perpendicular. If a great and artistic photographer had had to choose as to the best means of getting a really accurate and comprehensive likeness of Mrs. Penelope Broadbent, it is probable that he would have decided on a bird's-eye view as having many points of advantage.

The lady, although of somewhat ardent complexion, affected the most delicate conceivable shades of dress, probably by the way of contrast. The latter was certainly sufficiently startling. On this particular evening the dress which sheltered and adorned, without qualifying, the tropical super-abundance of the bishop's greater half, was a delicate primrose satin, and it shimmered and billowed in the softened light like waves of embodied chastity, while above it rose and fell a tossing wave of glittering jewels, the Broadbent historic gems, the envy, it was said, of Royalty itself.

The Bishop's lady, as became her rank, sat at the right hand of the host, while her benign and dignified lord sat next to the hostess at the bottom of the table.

How it came about will probably never be known with absolute accuracy, but just as a staid and dignified footman was about to hand a plate of turtle soup to Mrs. Broadbent, the gentleman on her right—our friend Mr. Felix Johnstone—was observed to be searching wildly for his handkerchief. Alas! unfamiliarity with the geography of pockets in dress clothes, and a hazy recollection that a table napkin should never be placed to the nose, and the result was that Mr. Johnstone's sneeze—a thing known and dreaded along a hundred miles of Australian coast—burst upon the dinner-table like the crack of doom. So weird, so awful, so unspeakable, and ear-splitting a sneeze had surely never been heard since the world began!

The footman, on Mr. Johnstone's left, utterly demoralized, dropped his plate of soup where he stood, by the chair of the Bishop's wife, and the contents, rich, dark, tenacious, fell on the ripe, warm shoulders of the shrieking, half-scalded victim, and rolled in an oily river down the palpitating, outraged bosom, and all athwart the delicate, primrose tinted garment.

The scene now beggared description. Mr. Felix Johnstone, also bespattered by the waiter's munificence, for which he was devoutly grateful, as it gave him an excuse for leaving the table, walked to the door as if he expected to be hanged outside. As he bowed himself out with a calm born of the supremest desperation, three glances were daguerreotyped on his brain—the flaming visage of the Bishop burning with a look of very unapostolic rage; the amused and cynical smile of Mr. Elphinstone Howard ("I've seen you before, where?" flashed the thought and inquiry through the unhappy one's brain), and last, a look of distress and commiseration directed toward him by Lady Evelyn. That last glance was one of resuscitation in its effects, and was painful, as such always are.

"O the pity of it!" the unhappy man murmured. "But for this awful occurrence she might have grown to care for me, but no woman ever forgave a man for making himself so ridiculous."

"Jarvis," he shouted as he entered his rooms, "bring me Bradshaw's Railway Guide."

"Yes, sir, I see you have had an accident, won't you change your clothes, sir, before you return to the dining-room?"

"Jarvis, you are an idiot, do I look like a man who is about to return to a dining-room? I want you to find me the earliest train that starts for the North Pole, and if you don't catch it, you'll catch something else; that, I can promise you."

Jarvis was a discreet servant of vast experience, and the train which he did look up, found its terminus in Euston Square, London.

"There is no train to-night, sir," was all he said, as he closed his Bradshaw.

An hour later Dick, the son and heir of the family, entered his friend's room, and after carefully closing the door and seeing Jarvis out of the way, he sat down opposite his friend and gave himself up to great and unrestrained laughter—laughing until the tears ran down his cheeks and until he rolled off his chair through weakness.

"The sight of that old girl!" he exclaimed irreverently between his paroxysms, "will last me till I die. She was clothed with soup as with a garment, and had more on than I ever saw her wear before at table. By Jove, Johnstone, you have rendered yourself immortal."

"That's right, old man, laugh your fill; but all the same, the thing has done for me. I shall leave here in the morning."

"Now look here," returned Dick with an approach to gravity in his manner; "that is precisely the very thing you must not do. My brain is small, but what there is of it is clear, and I know just what is going to happen. By to-morrow morning every one concerned in the accident, and most of all the Bishop and his wife, will be anxious to have the whole thing forgotten, and everything placed on its old footing. That is their only chance of escaping being made the laughing-stock of every county meeting within a hundred miles. Fancy it's getting wind that you had run away because you had been the means of having the Bishop's wife smothered with turtle soup while in a very *décollète* condition! Why, people would say it was judgment on the exuberant old dame. No, old chap, stay where you are and I'll guarantee you absolution both from Bishop and dame."

The other sat in silence for a while, and presently Dick continued, "By the way, if it is not too delicate a question, was there any special cause for that unique sneeze, and is that about your usual figure?"

The other winced for a moment, and then slowly answered, "That sneeze is my infirmity, but it does not spring from a cold. Ever since my earliest recollection the smell of musk has caused me to sneeze in just that way, and I noticed the scent of that perfume at table just before the attack came on. I was told in Australia that a very slight operation on the nostril, if skillfully performed, would cure the tendency to sneeze, and I thought I would try some specialist in London, but it is so long since I had one of the spasms that I imagined I was outgrowing them."

Mr. Johnstone's reception the following day bore out his friend's prophecy. The Bishop and his wife were cordial in the extreme and by common consent the unwelcome subject was tabooed. Indeed the affair was overshadowed by an occurrence of a much more serious character.

Mrs. Broadbent's jewels, to which reference has already been made, were discovered to have been stolen during the night. The shock which followed the announcement was intensified by the discovery that other jewels were missing. The stolen gems had been locked in a despatch box which was kept in the dressing-room adjoining the Bishop's bedroom, and in the morning the box was found open and rifled of its contents. As the diamonds taken were of immense value it was deemed advisable to send to Scotland Yard for a London detective, and a telegram had been received promising the arrival of the detective the following morning.

In the closer companionship which crime always induces

among the innocent within its orbit, Mr. Felix Johnstone found opportunities of conversation with the Lady Evelyn Beeton, and it is a pleasure to note that the lady found many solid attractions in the Colonist. He was different from the men of her acquaintance—more natural, more manly, less frivolous—in a word altogether more acceptable as a companion than her more polished friends.

In the result our hero sought his couch that night with very different feelings from those with which he had encountered it the previous night.

"About the North Pole, sir?" Jarvis had inquired, and his master's reply was, "Jarvis, if you mention that vegetable or mineral again, you'll lose your place. You leave that pole alone!"

And presently he slept the sleep of the just.

It was probably 2 A.M. when the door of Mr. Felix Johnstone's bedroom opened softly and a male figure stole in on tiptoe. The light burned low in a night lamp, but that did not embarrass the intruder, who carried a dark lantern of his own. The sleeper's face was turned from the door, and his breathing was deep and regular. Poising himself on his tiptoes, as if ready either to advance or fly, the intruder paused for a moment and regarded the sleeper attentively. Apparently the scrutiny was satisfactory, for the burglar now advanced noiselessly in his list slippers to a stout portmanteau, and as he laid his hand on the lock he murmured, "I know him of old; he always carries heaps of money with him." The better to facilitate his operations he laid a jewelry case, which he was carrying in his hand, on the dressing-table, while he took a bunch of skeleton keys from his pocket. With the keys a cambric handkerchief was drawn out, and instantly the room was filled with a pungent odor of musk. The subdued jingle of the keys, or some other influence, troubled the sleeper, who moved uneasily. Warily the burglar stooped over him with the aromatic handkerchief, which he had just picked up, in his hand. Instantly the closed eyes opened wide, and ere the burglar could even move his hand there burst on the silence of the night that stupendous and unearthly sneeze. It had seemed terrible beyond measure in the crowded noisy room; but here, in the midnight silence, its intensity and immensity baffled all description.

Instantly Johnstone, now fully awake, bounded to his feet, and being nearer to the door than the burglar, he shut and locked it, and turned to confront the intruder, who in his affright and surprise had turned the light of his dark lantern on the room and on himself. "Whew!" exclaimed the astonished Australian, who recognized in the man before him not only the elegant Howard Elphinstone whose face had puzzled him long, but also Red Winthrop, a notorious Melbourne burglar, whom he had once been the means of "sending up" for a term of years.

"Don't you think you have tempted your luck once too often, Red Winthrop?" inquired Johnstone grimly, as he faced the other with the bed between them.

The other's eyes gave a dangerous gleam, but he said nothing. He only shook his wrist sharply, and a long bowie-knife lay in his palm. But for an instant, however. The next moment it flew with unerring aim at the other's throat. Perhaps Johnstone should have been more on his guard, still his quick eye noted the danger, although not in time altogether to avert it. The willing blade hewed a deep rut along the side of the jaw, missing the jugular vein by a hair's breadth, and passing on went straight through a pier glass and stuck quivering in the wood at the back of the glass. As the latter shivered, Johnstone, unmindful of his wound, called out "Seven years' bad luck for you, Winthrop," and vaulting across the bed he closed with the ex-convict, whom, after a short but sharp struggle, he succeeded in tying, hands and feet.

Meanwhile the whole household, aroused by the unearthly noise, was pounding at the door. When the latter was opened, a combined scream burst from the assembled guests.

Johnstone was standing over the ex-convict in a pool of his own blood, which stained the white bed-clothes and even the walls of the room.

Little more will suffice. The casket left on Mr. Johnstone's table contained the Lady Evelyn's diamonds stolen that night. In the prisoner's rooms were found Mrs. Broadbent's jewels intact, and also those stolen from the other visitors.

Mr. Johnstone was in danger for some time from the excessive loss of blood, and when finally he managed to leave his room he did so, not only to find himself a general hero to all the folks at the Hall, but a very especial and particular kind of a hero to a certain Lady Evelyn Beeton.

When in process of time the mutual admiration between these two was crystallized in a happy union, the worthy Bishop tied the knot with an unction as ripe and gracious as ever the church sanctioned, while madame beamed on the alliance with a radiant effulgence which eclipsed and dwarfed all the surrounding objects.

Shortly after the recovery of our Australian friend he testified against Red Winthrop, and as that talented gentleman received his sentence of seven years' transportation, Mr. Johnstone dryly remarked, "You shouldn't break looking-glasses, Winthrop; I told you it meant seven years' bad luck."

It is only right to add that although our friend the Australian had sneezed himself back into favor after sneezing himself out of it, he rightly felt that so fateful a blast was a dangerous and uncertain possession, and, after a time, he took competent advice on the subject with the result that he now no longer dreads the musk odor which used to be his *bête noir*.

TWO CHRISTMAS EVES.

The swirling, eddying wind drove with a silent, ghostly fury up the deserted High Street of Upper Medlock one winter's evening in 1884, carrying with it into every crevice and corner, in its wild pirouette, great waves of heavy inch-square snowflakes.

"Oh, what lovely weather for Christmas time," exclaimed Mrs. Cargill as she stood by her husband's side looking out of the deep, broad, comfortable bow-window of their house on the rioting tempest in white outside.

"Do you know," she continued, nestling so close to her husband's side that he had to put his arm round her dainty little waist to maintain his equilibrium, "do you know, that a storm like this makes me think our new home doubly comfortable and beautiful. You see it is the first real home that I was ever able to call my very own or yours, dear, which is quite the same thing, is it not?" and she looked up into her husband's face with bright, happy eyes.

By way of reply her husband imprinted a warm kiss on the tempting lips so near to his own, and his arm tightened lovingly round the slender form.

"For shame, sir, kissing me at the window, I'm sure Mr. Strangely over the way at the banks saw you; it is too public even in a snow-storm."

But the husband dropped the arm which imprisoned her waist, and turned from the window with a sigh which only a strong effort kept from changing into a groan of despair.

"Ben!" exclaimed the anxious voice of his wife as she heard the sigh, "there is something wrong with you, tell me what it is, darling."

"No, dear, there is nothing wrong; I was standing in an awkward position that was all," and with this love-framed fiction the husband stroked his wife's glossy brown hair, and looked tenderly into her eyes. But there was a shade of wistfulness in his own which the wife's keen gaze noted with apprehension, and with womanly persistence she pressed her point.

At last, and not altogether unwillingly, for the load was a heavy one for a single heart to bear, the husband unbosomed his trouble, as, half an hour later, they sat round the bright fire, with the bleak storm barred and curtained out.

"You remember," he began, "how your rejected admirer, Banker Strangely, returned good for evil, as we thought, by giving me an opportunity of going into the Longfellow mining deal with him, by which he said we both would make an enormous fortune."

Mrs. Cargill nodded her head by way of reply, but kept silent. Her woman's wit already saw trouble ahead, but she anticipated it by no word.

"Well," her husband resumed, "you advised me not to have anything to do with the banker or his scheme; and, dear, you were so positive about it that when Strangely over-persuaded me by explaining that your objection arose only from a dislike to him, I felt averse to confessing what I had done until the money should have been made and I could bring it in my hand to you. You will recollect, dear," almost pleaded the husband by way of excuse as he looked into the loving, patient eyes before him, "we were not very well off, and," with a moist tenderness in his eyes, "I wanted so badly to have a pretty cage for the bonny bird I had just caught."

The hand on his own pressed it gently, and there was a soft mist rising in the corner of the brown eyes, but the mouth was set and firm.

"Tell me, dear."

The words fell from her lips, and they almost startled the husband, they sounded so unlike her usual soft, flute-like notes.

"Well," resumed the husband almost desperately, "the sum I was to put in was $10,000, which was just $5,000 more than I could command at the time. I told Strangely that, and he said he would let me have the other $5,000, on my note of hand, which, he said, could be paid out of the profits of the mine, which was then doing remarkably well. I hesitated about giving the note, but Strangely showed me a letter from the owner of the mine, a man named George Williams, of Denver, which stated that the preceding month's profit had been $1,500 nett, and he thought that figure would be maintained and considerably increased. Well, if that was true—and Strangely vouched for Williams' honesty—I could easily meet the note which he asked me to give, out of the profits, more especially as the banker said he would agree to let all the profits be put aside for that purpose, and would not himself draw anything until the note I was asked to give was paid.

"That same letter of Williams which I speak of showed me that since Strangely had paid $1,000 down to bind the purchase, he (Williams) had received an offer of $35,000 for the mine, which was $10,000 more than we were going to pay for it.

"So to cut a long and miserable story short, I gave the banker my note six months ago, and the purchase of the mine was completed, I contributing $10,000 and Strangely paying $15,000. Since that time we have had the hardest kind of luck with the mine. First of all the manager left; then the mine was flooded; then some of the wooden supports gave way, and one of the shafts was closed, and the end of it all is that we have not received a single cent from the mine since we took it over, and my note for $5,000 is due to-morrow, and all the money I have or can control is $200. Was there ever such hard luck?"

For a time the two sat in silence hand in hand, he, just a little bit averse to forcing a premature expression, she, with her soft velvety eyes staring unseeingly into the blazing coals, miles deep in thought. Presently she spoke, and her voice was sweet and even, but there was an icy air about it, as if the breath which uttered it partook of the chill of the dismal night outside.

"And Mr. Strangely, won't he enable you to meet that note or let it stand over, or renew it?" There was a suspicion of contempt in the last words, but not contempt for the person she was addressing.

"No, dear, Strangely has been telling me all the month that he is very short himself and that his directors will insist on the note being paid when due. He says that they have made some losses lately and are in quite a bad mood over them."

"Well, dear, but if you *cannot* meet the note, what will they do then?"

"They will protest my note, get a judgment against me, and sell my property.

"What! this house—our home!" almost screamed his wife, as she sprang to her feet, her indignant eyes all ablaze and giving back flame for flame with the leaping sea-coal fire.

"Yes, darling," murmured the weary, heart-broken man, "everything down even to the baby's cradle."

"O, but they *cannot* do it," replied the wife, her bright head high in the air, and her eyes full of a lovely defiance. "Ben," she resumed with a pitiful attempt at a cheery smile, "they cannot sell *you*, can they?"

"No, sweetheart," replied Ben with a duplicate of the same wintery heartbreaking mirth in his tone.

"Then never mind, my darling, love will find a way out of the difficulty. My poor, poor dear, to think that you have been bearing this burden all alone for these long, miserable months while I was so blindly, so foolishly happy. And, oh me! to think of a note falling due on Christmas eve; that must have been Mr. Strangely's doing that, to spoil our Christmas, now wasn't it dear?"

"Well, I tried to put it off till January, but he said he could not make the note for more than six months, although he could renew it. Now, of course, he says he cannot renew it."

"Just so, Ben, dear; do you not remember it was last

Christmas eve Mr. Strangely proposed, and I declined his suit? Does not this seem like what you call getting even with us, darling, just a little like that, eh? He is a vindictive, jealous man, and he has tried to ruin you, that is all, love; that mine was a complete fraud, just his way of wrecking *you*. Depend on it, I am right. Did you send anyone to examine the mine? Do you know positively that he put $15,000 into it? No, my own honest, unsuspicious husband, I see you did not. Well, be assured it is as I say, and although he has spoilt our Christmas eve, he will not spoil our lives or our love. A woman always gets a keen insight into the character of the man who loves her; that is, provided she does not love him. When she returns his love, she is blind and can see none of his faults. I saw a good deal of Mr. Strangely, and I always disliked him, even when he was expressing the greatest devotion to myself; he is a bad, unprincipled man. That is probably not just what the commercial agencies say about him, but I know I am nearer the truth than they are."

At this moment a ring was heard at the outer bell, and Mrs. Cargill rose hastily to her feet exclaiming—"Oh, that must be my brother Wilfred. I forgot to tell you that I had a dispatch from him this afternoon saying that he had arrived in New York from Denver, and would be here by this evening to spend his Christmas with us. I have not seen Wilfred for more than five years, and am so glad he is come. He is awfully cheerful, and will keep us from moping, and he is so lucky to everybody but himself, poor boy. He is quite poor, and yet he has been the means of making many people rich. He always seems to bring me good luck; and have you not seen people, dear, who were, on the contrary, what is called 'ill-fated,' who were always trying to do people good, and always harming them quite badly. No!—oh I have, time and again; and don't you remember, in Bulwer Lytton's 'Harold,' the ill-fated Haco, who is always trying to do the king good with the most disastrous results, and is finally the means of his death? Oh, I am so glad Will has come, and he is such a good hypnotizer too;" and so the dear little wife rattled on inconsequently, as if eager to drive out all miserable thoughts from her husband's mind. But with all her semblance of cheerfulness there was a certain hardness of outline about the rounded cheek and chin which was not noticeable before, and seemed out of place in one so young.

Presently her brother Wilfred was ushered into the room, and introduced to her husband. When the first hearty welcomes were over and the evening meal had been discussed, Wilfred entertained his host and hostess with a graphic account of his experiences in the far West. These exhausted, his sister inquired of him how he had prospered in his affairs.

"About the same as usual," was his response. "Still a bachelor and likely so to remain, for I am never more than $500 ahead of the world. I take my pleasure as it comes, and don't hoard up so that I may have it when I am older and less able to enjoy it."

The new-comer was a man of the most acute perceptions, and he soon became aware of a heaviness or constraint in the social atmosphere which pained him more almost than words could tell. "Great heavens," he murmured to himself, "I hope my sister Nell has not made an unhappy match; yet I cannot imagine Ben to be an unkind man. There is more here than meets the eye. I must get it out of him; it won't do to receive any confidences from her, if I am to make any use of them." He looked so abstracted in his musings that his sister, brightening up forcibly, said, "Why, Will, you are positively dull; are you busy hypnotizing someone now in the distance?"

"No," replied the brother with a smile, "the fact is I am a kind of wild, unregenerate creature whose habits get away with him at times, having no wife to regulate them, and I am craving for a cigar with all the force of a weak and vicious nature. If you have a den where I can tame this wild beast within me—for I smoke weeds of the vilest strength—I will come back in an hour clothed and in my right mind."

This was but a ruse to enable him to be alone with his brother-in-law, so that he might, if possible, induce or force a confession from him as to the cause of the domestic cloud. "Give me an hour with Auld Nick," growled Wilfred to himself, "and I would wring the inside combination of the doors of Hades out of him."

When the two men emerged an hour later from the cozy smoking-room, Wilfred knew all the facts of the domestic tribulation, and beyond an appearance of occasional absent-mindedness, bore the confession cheerily.

"What about Dick Strangely, who was formerly teller in the bank over the way, and one of your numerous and most persistent admirers, Nell?" he inquired.

"Why," hurriedly remarked his brother-in-law, "did I not tell you that he was president of the bank over the way who held my note."

"No, you certainly did not. Now Nell, your good husband has told me all about his trouble, and I want your opinion about it. You used to be pretty clear-headed; perhaps, however, I ought to have said pretty *and* clear-headed."

"And so he occupies the flat over the bank, does he?" was the inquiry which followed his sister's opinion expressed in womanly fashion, but with a sense and directness which caused the listener to weigh well every word that fell from her lips.

As he made the inquiry, Wilfred rose from his seat, parted the heavy window curtains, and, undoing the wooden shutters, gazed across the street. The storm had abated, and for the time being, at least, the snow had ceased to fall. The bright lamp-light from the street fell full on the massive front of the bank and showed a white face and cruel merciless gaze turned on the house —the house the Cargills were occupying.

"Why that was Strangely himself, was it not?" remarked Will, and the other nodding his reply he added, "Not much of friendship in that glance, brother-in-law mine; what do you say?"

Half an hour later the new arrival begged permission to retire, on the plea of fatigue. He had previously urged his sister to give him a bedroom in the front of the house, if possible. "I want to study the banker," he explained, "and I cannot think properly of anyone over my shoulder, or through a number of empty rooms." In kissing his sister he whispered in her ear, "I think things will come all right in time for Christmas eve." For a moment she brightened up and then with a little doleful sigh she replied, "Ah! you do not know how vindictive that banker is; he is working for revenge, not money."

"I know, I know," returned her brother with a touch of impatience. "Still you just believe what I say, and go to bed in peace. Leave things to me; I have straightened out worse tangles than this."

When his sister had left the room he drew a chair in front of the clear wood fire that burned in the low grate, and drawing to his side a small table, he leaned his elbow on it with his outspread fingers supporting his temples. For fully an hour he remained in that position, as immovable as if cast in bronze. At the end of that time he rose from his chair pale and almost ghostly in appearance, but with eyes that shone supernaturally large and bright against the white skin of his face. There was an air of set tension about the man, which a child would have recognized and a thick-hided crocodile of the Ganges have given the right of the road to.

The fire had faded away to smouldering, unnoticeable embers, and the lamp which had been turned down since his sister left the room was now blown out. Moving with a stride of extraordinary expression for the life and vigor the step conveyed, Wilfred stepped to the window, pulled back the curtains, drew up the blind, and swiftly but noiselessly raised the window. The bank across the way lay buried in repose. It was now 11.30, and to all appearances the inmates of the dwelling apartments over it were all in bed, and presumably asleep. The storm had abated, and only the dark unstarred sky above and the snow beneath recalled the storm which had so recently rioted through the street.

Wilfred's air, as his burning eyes rested on the bank building—or rather pierced it, for that was the impression their fierce intensity conveyed—was one of the most imperious command. It was no lifeless brick and mortar which those compelling orbs transfixed, and which the moving but voiceless lips ordered to perform their behests. His was a face for the deadly breach or the forlorn hope, and it grew paler and paler beyond even the pallor of death; while in spite of the gusts of icy air which swept in through the open window, the dew gathered, beaded and broke on his forehead, and mounted the stiffened hair that rose from his scalp like a frozen crest.

It was evidently no ordinary creature with which this ghostly and fantastic struggle was being waged. After the first stern bout and victory, there was a cessation of action for a few minutes, but soon a new struggle commenced, in which the stern monitor's visage became that of unbending command and insistence. There was threat, too, in the eye, threat of dangerous and instant action.

At this point the watcher seemed to look for some noticeable event in the house opposite, and surely enough, as if in instant obedience to his wish, the flicker of a lamp could be seen descending the stairs of the bank building.

Presently the light drifted into the bank itself and inside the railing of the president's office. Then slowly, and as if in a dream, the bearer could be seen to open the great iron safe and take from thence a portfolio, from which he carefully selected a document and then returned it to the safe. At this juncture a night policeman saw the light in the bank and hurried across the street preparatory to sounding an alarm. Recognizing the

President, however, by the light of his lamp, he desisted, and stood for a few minutes watching his movements. As he saw him enter his office and commence to write a letter at his desk he resumed his round, merely muttering to himself: "Pretty late for banking business, but I presume he forgot something."

Returning on his beat half an hour later he saw the banker emerge from his house, walk across the way and drop a long envelope into the letter-box of the house opposite, and then slowly and wearily re-enter his house.

Ten minutes later and the light died out from the banker's dwelling. Simultaneously a man, spent and exhausted beyond the possibilities of ordinary or even extraordinary fatigue, closed his window, sank into an arm-chair, and lay there with white upturned face, from which the perspiration dropped in big, round, ice-cold beads. Few would have recognized in the pallid face, carved by deeply hewn lines, the gay debonair countenance of Wilfred Wharton, the wit, *bon vivant* and *bon camarade* of the plains and city alike.

The following morning Wilfred was up betimes notwithstanding his exhausting labors of the night before. As he descended to the breakfast-room he met his sister, to whose inquiry as to whether he had been able to devise any means of escape from their desperate situation, he nodded encouragingly. "But," he continued, "you must get me the key of your letter-box at once before your husband comes down. It is necessary for the success of my plans that I control your correspondence for a few hours."

Within the letter-box he found a long envelope bearing the printed name of the bank. This he promptly opened, and after carefully perusing its contents, nodded in a satisfied way, and placed it in an inner pocket of his coat. Then returning the other letters unnoticed to the box, he carried the key upstairs to his sister.

At breakfast nothing was said of the subject of the note

due that day, but as soon as the servant had left the room, Wilfred plunged into the subject.

"Now, Ben," he began, "you have got to follow me blindly in this matter, or I cannot help you. If you agree to do that, I believe I can get you out of this mess all right. The first request I have to make is that you leave town for the day, without having any communication whatever with the bank. You may return in good time for dinner, and I will promise to report in full to you then. Now, as for you, Nell, if they send across for Mr. Cargill from the bank just say your husband is out of town for the day and will not be back till the evening; and tell them you know nothing about his business. I am going out of town myself and will not be back till five o'clock."

As the morning wore on there might have been seen a look of vast perplexity and uneasiness on the face of Banker Strangely across the way—that is to say, while in the privacy of his own room. At ten o'clock, on going through his private portfolio, he was unable to find the $5,000 note of hand of his "dear" friend Benjamin Cargill, due that day. He had spent an hour looking for it, and still finding no trace of it he sat down to consider the situation. The day before he recollected destroying some old private papers taken from the same portfolio, and although he had been exceedingly careful, he now came to the conclusion that he must have destroyed the note among those papers. The thought of being baffled of his revenge against Mrs. Cargill for her former slight—for, as the lady rightly surmised, it *was revenge* and not friendship which inspired the banker— consumed his very soul with rage. Was he to be thus thwarted after tracking his victim down? Not while his brain performed its accustomed office.

Taking pen in hand he wrote the following letter to his "friend" Mr. Cargill:

"Dear Sir:—

"I beg to remind you that your note for $5,000 in my favor is due here to-day. As I explained to you, if the amount is not paid by three o'clock the note will go to protest. I shall be very sorry indeed to have to resort to such measures, but for the reasons already given you, I have no alternative."

The reply which was brought back was: "Mr. Cargill is out of town for the day; the letter will be handed to him on his return."

This indicated either a neglect or indifference of the banker's intentions, which made the latter furious. "I wonder where on earth that note is," he remarked under his breath feverishly again and again. And as the day passed he grew half crazy with rage. At 2.30 he rang his bell for his signature-book and after opening it at the letter "C," he carefully studied the specimen signature given there by Mr. Cargill when he opened his account. Then from an inner drawer he took a promissory note blank and slowly filled it in, using for the purpose a bottle of stale black ink. "It is not forgery," he murmured, as if excusing himself to his conscience, "it is only justice."

Ten minutes later he rang his bell, and sent the note into the general office with instructions that if it were not taken up by three o'clock, the teller should take it across to Mrs. Cargill and see her about it. Then if still unpaid, he directed that the note should be protested.

The note being unpaid, the teller called on Mrs. Cargill, who politely informed him that she knew nothing about her husband's affairs. "Did she not seem anxious and perturbed when she saw the note?"

"No, sir, she looked at the handwriting quietly and inquired who signed her husband's name to it."

"What!" snarled the banker, "what did you say?"

"She inquired who signed her husband's name to the note, and I replied of course he signed it himself, and she said, 'Well, I think I ought to know Mr. Cargill's signature, and I never saw it as shaky as that before; he must have been put out when he signed that document.' "

When the teller retired, the banker sank into his chair in a heap as one who had received a death wound. "Great Heaven," he ejaculated, "what am I doing, is that woman going to drive me to perdition? But no, her remarks are only the silly talk of an ignorant woman. No one knows about the note being mislaid." Saying this he drove his hand down savagely on the gong on his table, and when the clerk appeared in response to his summons, he bade him in imperious tones to have "that note protested."

. . . .

At four o'clock a sleigh drove up to Mr. Cargill's house, from which Wilfred alighted after requesting the driver to wait for further instructions. Learning from Mrs. Cargill of the presentation of the note, Wilfred re-entered the sleigh, giving the driver fresh directions in a tone of command very unusual to him. After a drive of a mile the sleigh stopped at the house of a justice of the peace, for the second time that day.

On issuing from the house of the justice, Wilfred gave directions to be driven to the police station. After announcing his wishes there, he returned to his sister's house and finding her husband had returned he carried him off to the office of the Notary Public. At the latter place they inquired whether a note for $5,000 had been left there for protest that day. On learning that the note was in the notary's hands and would remain there until the morning, the Justice of the peace was again visited, and an hour later the notary was served with an injunction not to part with the note of hand.

Once more the sleigh's sweet bells jangled before the police station and when it sped on its way again its ample robe enfolded the sturdy albeit somewhat bandied legs of the night policeman whose acquaintance we have already made; but who was not now in uniform.

When Mr. Strangely returned to his residence from his own sleigh ride at 5.30 P.M., he was surprised to learn that three gentlemen awaited him in the parlor.

"Who are they?" he inquired of the servant, and when he learned that Mr. Cargill was one of the number he rubbed his hands together gleefully and murmured to himself: "At last, at last, I have got you in the toils, my lady with the dainty, devilish face that refused me so scornfully a year ago."

The look with which he entered the room where his visitors awaited him had a fine and scornful air of contempt about it, suggestive of unsatiated conquest, and slaves, male and female—especially female—dragging at his victorious chariot's wheel.

"You are come to take up that note, I presume?" he began, addressing Mr. Cargill and ignoring his companion, "but you are entirely too late. Honorable men do not come sneaking into a bank two hours after it has been closed and after their note has gone to protest. To-morrow the whole town will know that your note has been protested—no not to-morrow, for that is Christmas Day,—but you will be the talk of the town the following day, and no doubt *that* reflection will sweeten your Christmas dinner—as" he snarled through his shark-like teeth —"as your wife sweetened mine a year ago, through your accursed interference."

If he had not been carried away by his feelings he would have noticed the peculiar expression on the faces of his visitors, but he did not, and he raved on until, in a stentorian voice, Wilfred bade him be silent. What was it in the look and voice of that man that made the banker pause and wince as he met his gaze? "Who are you, sir, that dare——" he began, but his voice faltered, and his whole frame seemed to shrink as he met the other's full lambent eye bent upon him, and felt it thrilling him through and through.

"I know you, surely," he said slowly and almost feebly. "I have seen you before—somewhere," and then the other's gaze seemed to freeze him into silence.

"Listen to me, Banker Strangely, and do not dare to open your mouth till I have done."

"You have been engaged in a conspiracy to ruin my friend, Mr. Cargill. You induced him to give you $5,000 to invest in a mine named the Longfellow, near Denver, and give you his note for $5,000, and you told him you were paying $15,000 more, and that, you said, made up the entire purchase money. To insure his joining you, you showed him a letter from the manager of the mine named George Williams, showing that very large profits were being made. You knew Mr. Cargill's anxiety to make some money, so that his wife, who had had so many rich offers, might not pine for the wealth which might have been hers. O, revenge was sweet to you, and you played your cards well. Too well, my friend, for your own comfort now. You thought to wreck their happiness this fair Christmas eve, did you; well, there is going to be some wrecking done, my friend, but it is here in this house—*your* home—where it is going to occur and not over the way in the home of the woman you once said you loved.

"Your whole plot is laid bare. I hold in my hand in your own handwriting a full and detailed confession of your villainy which you wrote out last night and sent to my friend, together with the note for $5,000, which you acknowledged you had got from him by fraud. There it is, and see, you have endorsed it in your own handwriting, and added your private stamp to it. In the same letter you gave my friend the name of your accomplice, George Williams, and his address, and when I showed him your letter he confessed everything too, and told me a good deal more of your dealings than was needful for my case."

"It is all a lie, that letter is a forgery, I never wrote it, and that note was stolen from the bank last night," shrieked the banker, goaded to desperation, "I will send for the police."

"You need not send far, there is one outside the door," returned Wilfred. Then, opening the door, he summoned the officer to enter.

"This officer in private clothes is the policeman who was on duty last night, and saw you enter the bank office, unlock the safe, take out a document, and after closing the safe, write a letter which you enclosed in a long envelope and placed with your own hand in Mr. Cargill's letter-box. Am I not right, officer?"

"Entirely correct, sir."

The banker sat paralyzed, his brain benumbed with the extraordinary statement made to him. Was it all a dream, or was he going mad? And then like a flash of lightning he recollected inquiring that morning if the servant knew what had made his slippers so wet; it was the snow—the accursed snow, as he crossed the street to Mr. Cargill's. Ah! now he knew they were speaking the truth; besides, that was undoubtedly his handwriting and his seal; and that was beyond all question the genuine note.

"Then," resumed the inexorable Wilfred, mindful only of his sister's pain, "ignorant of what you had done in your sleeping hours and being unable to find the note which you had returned to its rightful owner, you imagined you had mislaid it, and lest your darling revenge for which you had imperilled your soul, should escape you, you forged a fresh note, which being of course unpaid, you have sent to the notary's for protest.

"Dick Strangely, you have played for a high stake—the wrecking of a happy home—and you have lost. That is all, this bright snowy Christmas eve! In my hand here I hold a warrant for your arrest on a charge of conspiracy with Williams to defraud Cargill, and also on a charge of forgery. I have obtained an injunction preventing the notary from parting with the forged note which he holds, and I have Williams safe in prison ready to bear evidence against you."

As one by one the banker heard of the steps taken to close every door against his escape, his head drooped lower and lower.

"Save me," he murmured brokenly at last, "I'm a poor, desperate, broken-hearted man, save me, and I'll make restitution."

As he glanced on the two faces beside him (the policeman had retired to the passage) he saw on the one, that of Cargill, a mingling of relief and amazement—for the revelations were not one whit the less surprising to him than to the banker—and on the other only relentless determination.

As he recognized the latter he sank on his knees and begged for mercy, offering to pay back double what he had defrauded his former friend Cargill of.

The two brothers-in-law stepped apart for a moment to confer. "Wilfred," urged the husband's voice, "this man was until recently a friend. He became an enemy because Nell refused him for me. Her rejection of his desperate love for her has made a scoundrel of him; I imagine it would have made a villain of me too. I surely can afford to be generous when I win all around. I cannot send a man I once called by the name of friend to jail on Christmas eve. Wait here, and I will go across and talk the matter over with my wife; she ought to be consulted on this business."

"Bring her here," was the laconic reply.

And so it happened that the mercy which Dick Strangely subsequently received that night was taken humbly and penitently from the hand of the woman he once professed to love, but whose husband and home he ultimately tried to ruin.

The banker returned the money that night of which he had defrauded his friend, and he also returned the mortgages. He offered indeed to pay back double, but his offer was refused with scorn and loathing.

Dinner at Mr. Cargill's was an hour late that night, but it was eaten with great joy and happiness of heart. "The happiest Christmas eve of my life," exclaimed Mrs. Cargill with eyes whose radiance was momentarily dimmed by their moisture; and so said they all.

"Wilfred," exclaimed the happy wife and sister as she rose from table to leave the two gentlemen to their after-dinner cigar, "I will never, never understand how you accomplished what you did. I believe you must have hypnotized Mr. Strangely. Did you, sir, tell me?"

"Perhaps," was the reply with a curious smile curling the outer wave of his moustache. "Ben, the port wine is with you!"

"Tell me, Wilfred, how you managed it," pressed his brother-in-law.

"Well," replied the other after a pause, "it is not fair to make me disclose the secrets of my success, but I had a good deal of influence over that fellow Strangely, at school. On one occasion I caught him at a very disgraceful trick and gave him a very memorable thrashing. After that he seemed to drift into my power somehow, partly by reason of his disgrace, which I kept to myself, and partly because a good thrashing is an excellent beginning in hypnotism among boys. As the result, I could make him do anything I liked. With such a ground-work I had no difficulty in bringing him under my influence last night, more especially as I have become a pretty successful hypnotist by long practice and study."

"Could you, do you think, have made him do what he did if you had not known him previously?"

"No, I think I would probably have had to go to work some other way with him, but I imagine he would have had to disgorge all the same. Hypnotism as an art is full of resources."

THE END.

GLANCING SHAFTS.

CHAPTER I.

THE place was Euston Square Station, the Metropolitan terminal depot of the London and Northwestern Railway; the hour 8:15 P.M. when from time wellnigh immemorial the London limited express has started for Scotland; the individual a tall, broad-shouldered man of, perhaps, twenty-five years, and known to the world, if not as yet to fame, as Richard Dalrymple.

As the traveller hurriedly took his seat in the first-class carriage which he had given the guard a couple of half-crowns to reserve for his exclusive use, he looked out with some impatience on a whole landscape of good-byes.

There were convivial good-byes perceptible in the refreshment department, there were lovers' good-byes "the world forgetting by the world forgot," then there were the multitudinous good-byes of good-fellowship. The universal parting injunction to "mind and write soon" was drowned in the hearty laughter and loud badinage which somehow or other appear to be inseparable from this station, possibly as a sort of counterpoise to the somewhat different style of off-going from the northern and sadder end of the line where the ties of friendship or kinship are apt to be closer and farewells longer and more affecting.

As Richard Dalrymple looked out upon the scene he thanked his lucky stars that there was no one there to bid *him* good-bye, and lest even a passing acquaintance should recognize him he hurriedly drew the window curtains and retired into the seclusion of his carriage.

"Thank God," he murmured to himself as the train moved out of the station, "I'm glad I'm off. It was safer to run away, she carries altogether too many guns for me."

As if to divert his mind from painful thoughts, he glanced out into the night and watched for a while, after an absent-minded fashion, the wayside stations as they fled past in endless procession.

Then an inbound express dashed by apparently smashing all the crockery of the world as it went, and the shock so far dislocated his ideas as to induce him to leave the window.

"I suppose I may as well make myself comfortable," he presently murmured to himself. "Barkirk is four hundred miles away and there is no change of carriages."

Saying this, he exchanged his tall hat for the regulation travelling-cap used in those ante-Pullman days.

As he uncovered his head, his clear-cut profile crowned with a profusion of light brown curls, such as ladies love to toy with, shone white and clear against the dark blue of the carriage upholstery.

"A strikingly handsome man both as to feature and complexion," all women vowed Richard Dalrymple at first sight — "and a manly-looking man, too," they were prone to add when they saw his width of shoulder and length of limb, and noted the frank fearless look of the well-opened dark blue eyes.

And yet as he opened his cigar-case to while away with "a weed," the tedium of the long hours, there was an air of anxiety perceptible on his brow and a worn look expressive of much turmoil and uncertainty of mind visible around his eyes, which, to all appearance, the joy he had expressed at his escape had not to any appreciable extent relieved.

As the dainty cigar-case of sweet-smelling Russia leather lay in his grasp a tender look came into his eyes, and opening the clasp, two lovely bunches of blue Scotch "forget-me-nots" lay before him worked in silk in marked relief on the soft lining of the case.

As he sat gazing at the small blue flowers a soft mist crept into his eyes and rose and rose until it blotted out both flowers and cigar-case and blurred the light blazing overhead.

Then from the innermost receptacle of his pocket-book he took a piece of soft tissue paper and extracted from it, with much tenderness, the half of a three-penny piece, which, after putting tenderly to his lips, he laid alongside the blue "forget-me-nots."

"It is just three years ago," he murmured to himself, "since Jeannie gave me these when I first left for London to try my hand at medicine there. I remember the very words of the old song which she repeated as she gave me the half of the broken coin:

'Now take this lucky thrupenny bit,
'Twill help you bear in mind,
A faithful, loving, trusting heart,
You left in tears behind.'

And although I have never seen my darling since, I have been true to her in word and thought and deed.

"Yes, indeed, I have," he repeated almost fiercely, as though someone had challenged his statement; and then, as if a twinge of remorse tortured him, he cried out, "Oh, forgive me, pet, if I have ever wavered, even for a moment; you know I have never loved anyone but you."

The heavy tears dropped from his eyes, and fell on the blue "forget-me-nots;" and then, as if ashamed to show his womanishness even to the walls opposite, he looked out into the night, through which the express now plunged on its furious way, rocking under its sixty-miles-an-hour gait.

Richard Dalrymple was what is termed a good, square man, and under the strongest conceivable temptation to prove himself a renegade he was doing his utmost, and not by any means with eye-service only, to prove himself true to his little Scottish sweetheart.

The cause—not of his apostasy, for he was still true in word and deed, and yes, in thought too, to his *fiancée*—but of his anxiety, was, all unknown to him, seated in the adjoining carriage with a smile of mingled triumph and apprehension lighting up her splendid dark eyes.

When Richard Dalrymple had regained his composure and had lit his cigar, the lady in the next compartment, detecting the odor, smiled again.

"Make yourself at home, *mon prince*," she murmured with a softer light in her brilliant eyes—"and good-night—a sweet good-night," she added tenderly, throwing a mute kiss with both hands in the direction of the invisible smoker. "The woman who loves you will keep watch over you, aroon."

CHAPTER II.

MISS Gwendoline Beattison, the lady who with her companion, an elderly Frenchwoman, occupied the adjoining compartment, was the daughter of General Beattison and of his wife, a Spanish lady of renowned beauty.

After acquiring great wealth in India, General Beattison—a Scotchman by birth—had returned to his native town, and there during the intervals of her visiting and education abroad his daughter had resided, and had made the acquaintance of Richard Dalrymple, the only son of Doctor Dalrymple, senior physician of the town.

When the younger Dalrymple had established a medical practice in the West-end of London it seemed only natural that the Beattisons, who generally spent from five to six months in the Metropolis each year, should patronize him, more especially as they knew him to be well trained in his profession, and well thought of among his brother practitioners.

Dalrymple was an attractive man, a good talker and possessed of a magnetism which drew other men to him. He was popular and was accordingly in demand and at no house was he more welcome than at the home of General Beattison.

But complications soon arose.

Mrs. Beattison had died while her daughter Gwendoline, an only child, was still in the nursery, and the latter's education had largely devolved upon governesses at home and abroad, whom her naturally dominant will soon reduced to subjection.

The result was that by the time she was sixteen years of age, Miss Beattison was a law unto herself, and it might be added with some show of truth, to her father also.

She was now twenty-one years of age and all the talk of "London-town," in her matchless beauty—the despair alike of painters and poets. From her mother she had inherited her black Castilian hair and glorious dark eyes, together with that magnetism of glance and capacity for arousing or manifesting passion which seems the heritage of Spain's seductive daughters.

From her father's side had sprung the height and stateliness which marked her carriage; and the unresting audacity of the warrior's blood was readily visible when Miss Gwendoline entered the lists.

Courted by all, and the belle of the London season, Gwendoline was true to an early—but undisclosed—infatuation for Richard Dalrymple, and with scant courtesy she refused the best offers of the season "by the score," bent upon securing the only being she had made up her mind she could love.

Richard, although by no means insensible to Miss Beattison's charms, was true to his Scotch *fiancée*, and feeling the fair Gwendoline's passion for him becoming more and more marked, and unable to see that he was holding his own satisfactorily, he deemed discretion the better part of valor and, as we have seen, fled.

Miss Beattison, who had fathomed his plans, determined to follow him, believing that only some mistaken notion of chivalry on his side kept them apart, and convinced in her own mind that they were made for each other, and wholly unwilling that both their lives should be ruined by a false delicacy on her part.

It will be seen that her views were very far indeed from being orthodox on the question of woman's rights, so far as they relate to courtship, but as against this it may be said that no breath of suspicion had ever been raised against her fair fame, and that her determination in following Mr. Dalrymple was consistent with a hereditary obstinacy in legitimate pursuits, once she was satisfied as to what was the right thing for her to do.

As Richard Dalrymple finished his third cigar the train was nearing Rugby station, its first stopping place.

"The preacher was entirely right," he muttered, as he threw away the end of his cigar; " 'fill a bushel full of wheat and there will be no room for chaff.' I have not been thinking enough of Jeannie, or this thing would never have worried me.

"The dear little darling," he suddenly burst out with a new accession of fervor, as he took a photograph from his pocket and kissed it again and again. "I will have a thousand copies of that photograph made, and I will put them everywhere in my house and study and in my pockets, so that people will say 'what a model lover he is!' and that will stimulate me to be still better than I am."

He kept on talking for some time until he became conscious of an undue earnestness in his avowals. "Great Heavens!" he suddenly exclaimed, "I hope I am not protesting too much—Oh no, no—how can I talk like that when I am within eight hours of the sweetest lips in Christendom, all mine too—exclusively—unkissed, unreaped for three years and just, just (here hyperbole failed him)—just too sweet for anything."

"Those lovely blue eyes, that rounded neck and that yellow hair, and those dear arms! O dear, I feel them now even after three long years.

"I hate dark eyes and black hair and all your over-ripe Southern beauty; I wonder I ever gave it a thought; it is so commonplace beside the charm of the ravishing blond."

In his excitement he had risen to his feet and was pacing backwards and forwards in his carriage, thrusting his arms out forcibly in front of him, as if in an effort to throw off excitement.

In turning, his hand struck the frame of the window forcibly, and the photograph fell from his grasp underneath the seat.

As he stooped to recover it he saw a handkerchief alongside it. This he at first mistook for his own until the softness of its texture undeceived him.

Rising to his feet he held the handkerchief somewhat carelessly to the light with the air of one who had nothing better to do, to see if he could discover any initials upon it. As he did so he became conscious of a subtle perfume, and it moved him horribly, as some men die without being moved.

His knees gave way through the weakness and he sat down. There was, he felt, but one person in all England who used that dainty Oriental perfume. She had told him so, and that one was herself.

Lest there should be any doubt as to the identity of the handkerchief, there, too, was the monogram in gold and black on the corner, the initials G. B. subtly intertwined.

In silence Richard Dalrymple sat with whitening face looking at the delicate piece of cambric in his hands.

"My God!" he suddenly burst out, "What is the matter with me; it is all I can do to keep myself from kissing it!"

His hand shook as it held the piece of vagrant cambric, and when the train entered Rugby station a man in the depths of self-abasement knelt on the floor of Dalrymple's compartment with his head buried in the cushions of the seat.

CHAPTER III.

WHILE the train was standing in the station at Rugby, and the majority of the male passengers were taking their last "night-caps" at the bar of the refreshment room, before composing themselves finally to sleep, a voice of somewhat uncertain fibre called to the guard as he passed the window of the carriage occupied by Richard Dalrymple.

"Guard, come here a minute. Can you tell me how that handkerchief got into this carriage?" and the speaker handed the dainty piece of cambric which he had found to the astonished guard.

Before the latter had time to frame a reply a shrill female voice from the next compartment called out, "Come here at once please, guard, quick!!"

The call was so urgent and the necessity of the caller apparently so desperate that, with a hasty "Excuse me, one moment, sir," to Richard Dalrymple, the guard stepped to the door of the adjoining compartment.

"Come inside please, guard, I've crushed my finger in the window and can't get it out."

As soon as the guard had entered the carriage the lady who had called him—Miss Beattison's companion—promptly placed herself in front of the door to prevent anyone from seeing inside, and then waved the guard toward her mistress.

"O, conductor, please tell me," said the other with great eagerness, "what the gentleman in the next compartment found. I overheard part of your conversation but not all."

"Well, miss, he found this handkerchief, and it seems to have startled him very considerably indeed."

"O dear, dear, it is one of mine which I must have dropped in that place to-night. You will remember that you showed us into that compartment first of all, but I exchanged it for this one because it gave me a better view of the entrance gate, and enabled me to see who was going off by train."

"Now, guard, that gentleman next door is a friend of mine, but I would not for all the world he knew I was near him; he would certainly want to travel in the same carriage, and that would be quite a nuisance.

"Tell him the handkerchief must have been left there by one of a party of Northern visitors to London and must have escaped the cleaner's notice.

"Be steady now and on no account let him suspect that I am in this carriage," and a small golden coin changed hands.

When the guard returned to Dalrymple the latter questioned him as to what was wrong next door. "Lady jammed her hand in the window, sir."

"Dear me, and did you raise the window and relieve her hand, poor thing."

"Well, no, sir—come to reflect, hang me if I think I did "—this with evident shamefacedness.

"You are a funny fellow, guard. After being called to open a window and relieve a suffering damsel, you come away not only without taking off the pressure, but you forget all about it; get out of my way and I'll attend to the suffering lady."

"Hold on, sir—stop, I say, stop!" called out the guard resisting the other's exit, "the lady's hand is all right now, and besides I haven't told you the worst, the lady is in a high fever and—and it looks like small-pox. I didn't want to tell you at first," he went on mendaciously, "but you have forced it out of me; please don't say anything about it or I'll get into trouble."

"Great Heavens!" ejaculated the traveller; "what an awful calamity! I wish you would stand a little further off. Suppose," he added under his breath, "I should carry the infection to Jeannie."

Then he added aloud as the other was leaving, "You have not explained how that handkerchief came to be in this carriage."

"Oh, that is a very simple matter, sir," replied the other promptly with an "in for a penny in for a pound" air, "a party of ladies came up to London in this carriage on my last trip, and I suppose one of them dropped her handkerchief under the seat, by accident. The name on their trunks was Bertrand, and I heard one of the young ladies called Georgiana, and the initials being the same," continued the guard giving full swing to his imagination, "I suppose the handkerchief belongs to her."

"That sounds all right," returned Dalrymple, giving a side glance at the piece of cambric as if he would have liked to have asked for it had he only known what excuse to make for his request.

Now as the lady in the adjoining carriage, anxious that our traveller should have a reminder of her, had with much and unwonted palpitation of heart, suggested to the conductor the propriety of returning the handkerchief to the finder, he had no particular difficulty in meeting the other's unspoken request.

"I suppose you may as well place that handkerchief where you found it," the guard remarked handing it to Dalrymple as he closed the door, "it is the usual way."

"Well, I suppose so," replied the other with affected indifference, receiving the precious article from his hands.

As the train sped on its way Dalrymple sat for a while with corrugated brow, then he suddenly muttered as he lit a last cigar before turning in for the night:

"That explanation might account for the initials, but how about the perfume? The coincidence is too striking. I don't understand it, and I believe that small-pox scare next door is all a trumped-up affair. I wonder who the people are who curtain themselves so closely in there, and what they mean by fooling the guard so."

He awoke once during the night to find himself with a photograph of his lady-love in one hand and the handkerchief in the other. This arrangement stung him to the heart, and he made as though he wanted to throw the handkerchief out of the window.

"But no!" he said to himself in time, "I might need it as a reminder that I must brace myself and drive all thoughts of Miss Beattison out of my mind."

That this reasoning was faulty was more than proved by the rapid softening of the severe glance which he directed towards the fluffy piece of cambric, which, as if half afraid of some necromantic influence, he held gingerly between his finger and thumb.

"Guard," he said, "I don't believe that cock-and-bull story about small-pox in the next compartment, or that high old tale you told me about the lady crushing her hand—now who *are* these people next door and what little game are they dragging you into?"

"I don't know anything more about them than I have told you," returned the conductor somewhat curtly, "and I've got too many daft people bothering me all the time without hunting up fresh ones."

Saying this he raised his silver whistle to his lips and blew a loud blast, at the same time waving his right arm up and down toward the engineer like a crazy semaphore; all of which was the signal to go ahead.

Dalrymple retired to his seat with a rather chagrined smile.

"Slightly personal, that remark," he said as he recomposed himself for sleep, "but I suppose he *is* worried quite a good deal by queer people. This line seems to be haunted to-night."

CHAPTER IV.

WHEN Dalrymple awoke again, dawn was breaking coldly and slowly among the mountains of the lake district.

When he put his head out of the window of his carriage, the fresh chilly air of the hills carried his memory back with a rush to his old Scotch days, and to the time of his courtship.

"Oh, my little pet," he murmured, turning to the photograph in his hand, "it seems but yesterday since you and I plighted our troth to each other on just such a hillside as this one here. I remember the smell of the heather that day, and how I could hardly find you a place to sit down on in the soft velvety sward, because you said you never liked to crush the bonny blue-bells—and they were all around us; and the lark, I recollect, rose from our feet and soared aloft, and we said it was singing us a wedding march.

"And that big intrusive bumble-bee too, that would fly around our heads—we could not bear to hurt it, we were so happy ourselves, and I have never even killed a wasp since for the memory of the time. Ah! and I remember too, Jeannie, the touch of your dear little hand so plump and firm, and the look in your bonny blue eyes when I told you I loved you and asked you to marry me; you looked so beautiful and shy.

"I was the happiest man on earth till that day, and there never has anything come between us, until now."

As he ended there was a sharp tone of anger in his last words, and rising quickly and with much energy he opened the window and threw from it with all his force the poor little piece of monogrammed cambric, which had been lying on the seat before him.

As this little incident culminated the train was slowing down to enter the small station where travellers to the Lakes break their journey, and a barefooted youngster who had run out to meet the train caught the feather-like handkerchief as it fluttered and eddied from the advancing train.

A lady sitting at the adjoining window which was open, heard the violent banging of the sash ahead and saw the handkerchief thrown forcibly out.

"Call to that boy instantly, madame, to give you that handkerchief."

The speaker was Miss Beattison, and as she made way for her companion at the window the natural pallor of her face became almost ghastly as she placed her hand to her side.

"Oh! *oh!* OH!" she moaned, "at last he has broken my heart. Now indeed I know how much he hates and loathes me by his throwing my poor little handkerchief out of the window as if it was infected by the plague. Oh how he must despise me!" Here gentle nature came to the relief of the sad-eyed, heavy-hearted sleepless one, and she burst into a flood of passionate tears.

"Has the boy got the handkerchief?" she inquired through her sobs.

"Yes, mademoiselle, here he comes with it, running alongside the train."

"Oh, take it from him quickly, dear," the sobbing maiden faltered, "or I think I shall die of shame and mortification."

"Boy, bring that handkerchief here, it belongs to me," shouted a commanding voice from the carriage ahead—and at the sound of it the tears in Miss Beattison's eyes stood still—a frozen cataract.

"The lady wants it, sir; she says it is hers," protested the boy.

"Oh, madame, slay that boy," said Miss Beattison in a fierce little whisper.

"The lady is mistaken, bring that handkerchief here at once."

"But it is a lady's handkerchief, sir," urged the boy.

"Bring it here at once, you little devil, or I'll break your neck."

Coarse words these, and oh how impolite to the other claimants, and yet sweeter far to the straining ears of the offended one than the softest music!

But the boy was "dour" in the face of ugly words or threats, and he held out the handkerchief to the lady at the window.

"No, no, give it to the gentleman," said madame, and after a moment's hesitation the boy threw the handkerchief into the carriage where Dalrymple was standing.

Dalrymple endeavored to reward the boy by throwing him a shilling, but the threat was not forgotten and the boy who came of a fighting stock threw the coin back into the carriage.

Dalrymple saw with surprise a coin of large dimensions fall into the boy's hands from the other window, and he lighted a matutinal cigar to try and cipher out the peculiar kind of lunatics there were imprisoned in that adjoining compartment.

As for the eventful handkerchief, as if he were ashamed of having had it brought back he let it lie where it fell.

Next door an unusual occurrence had already taken place. Rising to her feet and swaying to and fro in the excess of her emotion, and with her beautiful eyes swimming in happy tears, Gwendoline Beattison threw herself on the hard bosom (but not hard heart) of her old companion and friend, and murmured as she flung her arms around her neck, "Oh, it was all a mistake. He did not intend to throw away my handkerchief. Did you notice how furious he was, the darling, when he thought some one was going to take it, eh?" At which, by way of reply, the truthful companion groaned with much and genuine distress.

"I shall find out all about this mystery of the next compartment once I get to Carlisle station," muttered Richard Dalrymple to himself. "We stop there fifteen minutes for breakfast, and it will be strange if I can't find out what particular kind of asylum I have next door then."

Saying this he relit his cigar and gave his eyes to the

dreamy study of the Northern landscape, while his mind projected itself ahead to the meeting so soon to take place between himself and his sweetheart, from whom he had been parted for three long years.

But "the best laid plans of mice and men gang aft aglee," especially when it is a woman's wit which is the disturbing influence.

At the last station before entering Carlisle, Miss Beattison called the guard to her, and begged that he would find an empty carriage in the rear of the train (their carriage was now in front) for herself and companion, into which they could change the moment the gentleman in the adjoining compartment should leave it for his breakfast.

"But suppose he does not leave it?" gloomily queried the guard; "men who smoke so much in the early morning can easily wait for their breakfast until they get home."

"Well, in that case," responded the lady, "we will try some other plan, but this will do until we know it can't be carried out; and at Carlisle we will keep our curtains closed until you give us warning to change, in case he should feel inclined to satisfy his curiosity about us."

"By the way, guard," resumed the lady, after a momentary pause, and with a little tremor in the voice, "did you happen to notice what he did with the handkerchief?"

"Yes, madam, it is lying on the seat in front of him and he is studying a photograph."

"That is all, guard, thank you," returned the lady in a fainter tone, as she leaned her head back on the cushioned partition.

"You look faint, mademoiselle," said her companion, hastening to her side with an anxious look in her eyes—"will mademoiselle try a little sal-volatile?"

"Thank you, no," replied her mistress; "I think it is only that I am a little faint after my long night's travel."

She sat in silence for a few minutes while the companion watched the pallid face, and the white lids and long dark lashes which hid the beautiful eyes.

There was a saddened droop in the beautiful mouth with its gracefully curved lips, as if Cupid's bow had been bent just a little awry. And where, oh where, was that imperious look which was wont to be enthroned on that boldly rounded chin? The change was Love the humiliator's work.

The silken scarf thrown over the shapely head had fallen aside and now showed the beautiful hair in all the graceful abandon consequent upon a night's comfortless travel.

The dusky tresses with the wave of a wind-swept banderol in them grew low and luxurious over the broad white forehead, and curled upwards in wealthy profusion over the graceful head.

The beautiful and strongly marked eyebrows, the densely fringed lids and all the component parts of superlative beauty were there.

Men talk of alabaster loveliness, of faces pale and perfect as flawless marble, but these similes fell far short of Miss Beattison's complexion, which was the despair of the rest of the sex. In her case these would have been dead illustrations of a living glorious beauty to which neither nature nor art could furnish an analogy or an expression.

Her beautiful eyes, now closed in heart-breaking reflections, like her other perfections defied descriptions and beggared eulogy!

Even Byron, grand-master in the art of portraying woman's ravishing beauty, recorded his failure to describe the beauty of lovely eyes, and his words might well be appropriated for Miss Beattison:

"Her eye's dark charm 'twere vain to tell
But gaze on that of the Gazelle,

It will assist thy fancy well."

Suddenly the dark eyes opened widely, and the taper fingers clenched in a paroxysm of emotion.

"Oh, why should I waste myself upon a man who does not care for me?" she cried out bitterly. "What have I done that Heaven should grant me power to love only one man when it makes that man despise me, and prefer an ignorant Scotch country girl, whose love as compared with mine is as the shallow sea-shell to the bottomless ocean."

"Oh, mademoiselle, give him up—let us go back, he is not worthy of you; there are a thousand handsomer, cleverer men— distinguished men too—who would kneel at your feet to-morrow—yes, mademoiselle, and put proud coronets there too; and splendid men, too, ah! if the poor companion could but choose! there are some ravishing gentlemen who visit you, and think you that I would run after a country doctor and break my heart when all the great world would come to me? Ah, *mon Dieu*, no."

"Hush, madame," replied the other, "you do not know what you are talking about. I know—of course I know, and the thought drives me nearly crazy with rage against myself—that I am doing an indelicate and unmaidenly thing in following up Dr. Dalrymple. Oh, I have fought against this love on my knees— yes, on my bended knees—but I cannot help myself. I love him, *I love him*, I love him! Even when I wore short dresses he was, all unknown to him, the idol of my childhood. Yes, I used to dream about him and pray God to give me him for a dear husband when I grew up. I remember him as he used to come up the church aisle on Sundays, and as he passed our cross-pew I used to redden until I fancied all the people in the church knew about my love for him. And during the sermon I never recollected the text, or remembered what the old clergyman said, I was just thinking of Richard (that is what I called him in my mind) and longing to run my fingers through his bonny curly brown hair. And oh when his moustache began to grow, as soon as I noticed it I insisted on being put into long dresses so that I might, as it were, keep in step with him; and when I went abroad it was still the same all the years I was away; nothing ever took his boyish image out of my heart. I did not flirt and carry on like other girls, I just thought of him and waited, oh, so patiently! until my education should be completed, and I could return home practically my own mistress.

"Now, madame, do you think that love like that is going to stop because a thing seems unmaidenly, when all the happiness of my life is concerned in the result? Do you know that Dr. Dalrymple is now on his way to see his *fiancée*, and that this is the most crucial period of my whole life? Oh, if I were a man, and our positions reversed, I would carry him off!"

Madame was in despair—she held up her wrinkled hands and exclaimed again and again, "*mon Dieu, mon Dieu!*" and then her womanly heart coming to her aid, she took the beautiful head between her hands and kissed it again and again. "God is good," she said, softly but hopefully, "maybe it will all come right yet."

Large tears—the advance guard of grief's thunder shower which indicates but does not relieve the pent-up passion—gathered slowly and fell from Miss Beattison's eyes, and the white teeth tried hard to restrain the quivering lip. But the effort was in vain, the rising sob refused to be quelled, and unable any longer to restrain her emotion, Miss Beattison covered her face and sobbed out her very soul on her old companion's sympathetic shoulder.

"Ah," muttered the companion aside to herself, "if I were a man and had a knife I would kill you!" and she shook her clenched fist at the invisible traveller next door.

When Carlisle station was reached Dr. Dalrymple stepped quickly from his carriage, thinking to catch a glimpse of the inmates of the adjoining compartment.

The curtains, however, were closed, and no sign of life was visible.

"Asleep, I imagine," soliloquized the Doctor, "well, I suppose I may as well have some breakfast," saying which he sauntered in the direction of the first-class restaurant.

When he returned the window of the carriage next door was in the same condition. "Still asleep," he murmured as he lit his cigar, and the train moved outward.

Dr. Dalrymple was in error, however, for the change of carriage had been effected while he was at breakfast and his whilom companions were now a dozen carriages to the rear.

At the next station, the first on Scotch soil, noticing the adjoining door open, Dr. Dalrymple inquired of the guard if the ladies were still inside the carriage. "No, sir, they left at Carlisle," replied the guard, an answer literally correct and yet giving, and intended to give, the impression that the ladies had left the train at the station named.

"Well, well, I wonder who they were—something unique, I should say——"

"Yes, sir, quite so," said the guard as he left the door, adding to himself, "I seem to have more than the average of unique people this trip."

CHAPTER V.

WHEN Richard Dalrymple reached Barkirk he was considerably surprised to see General Beattison's carriage awaiting the arrival of the train.

"Some visitor to the old general," he surmised, adding under his breath with a long drawn sigh of uncertain meaning, "It really does look as if I was never to be allowed to forget that family."

The visitor, whoever it was, was slow to alight, and Dr. Dalrymple's hack drove off without his having cleared up the point.

The new arrival's welcome to his native home, after so long an absence, was the heartiest conceivable, and so thoroughly was he taken possession of, that it looked as if only by some desperate subterfuge would he be able to tear himself away to call upon the object of his affections.

And here it should be told that the engagement between Richard Dalrymple and Miss Jeannie Farquharson has been maintained as a profound secret by request of the latter, in order not to antagonize a wealthy and cantankerous aunt, her sole remaining relative. This state of affairs had limited the correspondence between the two, as their letters had to pass through the hands of a third person, who, knowing how cruel the tender mercies of a gossiping Scotch town are, did not care to receive too many lest she should arouse curiosity and set too many tongues wagging at her own expense.

At last, under pretence of a visit to his old friend Miss Farquharson the elder, Richard Dalrymple stood in the drawing room of Laburnum Lodge awaiting with a beating heart the arrival of his *fiancée*. The servant had said Miss Farquharson was out but would return in a few minutes, and would he see Miss Jeannie?

Would he! The gods were at last propitious!

When the servant went upstairs to announce his arrival,

he expected to hear, maybe, a little glad cry, and the instant rush of descending skirts.

But no, the house was still, and after a minute or two the servant returned to say Miss Jeannie would be down directly. For a moment the room seemed to grow chilly, but his face brightened and the temperature rose again when he reminded himself that no doubt she had heard of his arrival, and it was necessary for her still to dissemble her love before tattling servants.

Presently he heard the sound of a soft foot-fall on the stairs and the *frou-frou* of a lady's dress gliding downward from step to step. His heart beat faster, the color slowly left his cheek, and a happy expectant light shone in his eyes.

Yes, there, at last, the queen of all his hopes and joys stood in the doorway, not indeed the Scotch lassie of his recollection and his dreams, but a vision of fair Northern loveliness whose very perfection chained to his side the arms he had raised to embrace her, and nailed his feet to the floor; so that the passionate embrace of welcome which he had so often rehearsed in his own mind, all miscarried.

"Miss Farquharson—Jeannie—my darling!" he exclaimed with a faltering voice regaining control of himself and stretching out, not his arms but his hand, "I scarcely know you, you have grown so beautiful—what, what have you done with my shy little Scotch lassie?" Then he laid his hands on her shoulders and looked deep into her eyes.

Yes, they at least were the same, they had not changed while he dreamed of them these three long years, but they were not wont to droop before his gaze then as now.

Then his arms stole softly around the lissom waist, and gently and almost reverentially he stooped his lips to hers.

"Oh, please, Dick, don't," suddenly exclaimed the young lady with a struggle, and a rapidly rising color in the clear brown cheek.

"Why, Jeannie dear, what is the matter?" queried her lover in a distressed tone. "Don't you love me any longer, darling?"

"Oh no, it is not that, Dick dear," with faltering voice; "but we have been parted so long, and I've hardly got accustomed to you yet, you seem so formidable to me now, remember you were hardly more than a boy when you left; and now you have grown so big and strong and manly-looking, it doesn't seem at all the same thing to kiss you now."

"Well, darling, if that is all, the strangeness will soon pass, but dear me! this seems a cool meeting for lovers."

"Let us sit down, Dick, and talk things over," replied Jeannie, taking his hand and leading him to the sofa.

But Miss Farquharson's knock was heard at the door, and they had only time to hurriedly appoint a meeting for the following day at the lonely Granton Falls, when the elder lady entered the room.

Richard Dalrymple's mind was ill at ease during the rest of the day, and he was glad when the evening came around and he could have a confidential chat with the special friend and mentor of his old school days—Alec Douglas.

He determined to unbosom himself to his former "chum," and receive from him the sweet solace of his sympathy as in the days of yore, when he knew Alec to be as true as steel and the best secret-keeper in the world.

Richard explained at length to his friend his relations with Miss Jeannie Farquharson, but he was too much of a Bayard to allude to Miss Beattison's infatuation and its effect upon himself and his actions.

Alec Douglas sat silent while his friend unbosomed himself. He interrupted by no comment, but that he listened attentively may be gathered from the fact that his cigar went out unnoticed, and presently fell from his lips altogether without awaking his consciousness to the fact.

As his silence remained unbroken even after the close of the other's confidence, Dr. Dalrymple inquired what he thought of the situation. He fancied that the expression on his friend's face lacked the old-time sympathy he was wont to express, and yet that failed to qualify his astonishment when the other rose to his feet and after the merest pretence of looking at his watch, announced that he must leave to keep an appointment with a client.

"About your inquiry, Dick, as to what I think of the situation I can't say anything, but I consider that I am the last person you should ask such a question," saying which he strode out into the night.

"Well, I'm——blest if I don't think everyone has gone back on me since I left. My sweetheart is like an icicle and my old friend is as chilly as a Norway blizzard. I feel like Rip Van Winkle who outlived or outslept all his friendships.

"What did he mean, I wonder, about his being the last person in the world I ought to ask? Is he so proud of his legal reputation that he thinks it beneath him to give an opinion about a friend's love troubles? I suppose that is it, but if it is, this wretched little town hardens the heart worse than much abused London does."

CHAPTER VI.

RICHARD DALRYMPLE spent a restless night, and counted the minutes almost until it was time to meet his *fiancée* at Granton Falls.

He had some difficulty in evading his friends, but finally managed to be at the place of rendezvous some twenty minutes before the time fixed.

The place appointed was the corner of a stone bridge which spanned the Eildon river at Granton Falls, the said falls being simply a succession of small rapids.

As Richard looked over the bridge he noticed the footpath about fifty feet lower than the bridge, and said with some anxiety: "I hope Jeannie did not mean the footpath at the falls, for if she goes there while I am here I can't get to her without breaking my neck over those rocks."

At that instant the sharp ring of a horse's hoofs on the hard granite road aroused his attention, and turning round slowly, to his utter bewilderment, he saw Miss Beattison, unattended by her groom, reining in her horse by his side.

"How do you do, Doctor Dalrymple? Will you please help me to dismount, I have something to say to you."

Then she tied her horse to the nearest sapling, and came to his side; her face white and almost stern in its set expression.

"Are you wondering how I came to be here? Well I came by the same train as you did, to find out for myself whether the secret of your indifference to me was to be found here, in this little country town; and if it was the case, dear, as I had heard that you loved another, why, then, I determined I should end my most miserable life, for to me death is a thousand times better than life without you. Please do not think ill of me, for, as Heaven is my witness, this unrequited love is more than I can bear. This lonely walk what does it mean? Are you waiting now to keep some appointment?"

As Gwendoline Beattison stood before Richard

Dalrymple in all the pride of her splendid beauty, pleading the cause of her own desperate heart, his brain reeled before this fresh temptation. Did the struggle of all these long months and the resolution displayed in his flight count for nothing? Had he come all these long four hundred miles only to capitulate here? Perish the thought, and yet his breath came fast and faster as he gazed upon her, and his eyes faltered and fell before the terrible battery of hers. He held up his hands, palm outward, as a drowning man who finds the current too strong for him, and murmured, "Leave me. For God's sake go away and leave me."

That is what he meant to say—and perhaps it is what he did say—but every sense he had was surrendering to the irresistible usurper, and he could not be sure that even his speech was not betraying him.

He tried to think of Jeannie, but his very soul shook as if there, too, in the very holy of holies of his heart, a traitor was offering capitulation on the conqueror's own terms.

Every glance was a temptation to the stricken man as Gwendoline Beattison stood before him. Her closely fitting habit revealed every throb of the over-charged bosom and told all too plainly the tempest which was convulsing it. His own heart bounded madly in response, every fibre of his powerful frame thrilled in sympathy with the passion which shook the voluptuous figure before him, and his eyes no longer sought the ground but, alas!—*bon gré mal gré*—soon outdid hers in their fiery candor.

Words failed them both. It was the silence of the duel when the smallest flash of the blade may mean a life. As deadly was their silence and as vital, but their eyes—ah, their eyes spoke with a measureless volume and thrill, which deadened their ears to every earthly sound.

"Oh, why can't you love me, dear? am I so unattractive that you must run away from me?"

As Gwendoline Beattison said this, a wonderfully soft

and pathetic look came into her beautiful eyes, and, as if unable longer to control herself, she placed her two trembling hands on Richard Dalrymple's shoulders.

"Why is it, dear—won't you tell me?" and the voice which had been shaken by passion became strangely gentle and tender as the straying hands growing bolder stole around his neck and her beating heart in dire proximity fired his own anew.

Oh, Jeannie Farquharson why do you not hurry to the relief of your faltering lover, true to you so long in the face of a desperate temptation, but now, alas, in the toils!

Too late! the perfume which surrounded the fair temptress like an atmosphere was in his nostrils, the intoxication of her gaze mounted to his brain; her touch thrilled him to his finger-tips, his very soul tottered on its throne, and in another instant their lips met in a long clinging kiss—a kiss never to be undone, never to be forgotten, the kiss of a lifetime after which man and woman ought to die eternally, since in its rapture they have beggared Paradise!

The long ecstatic kiss ended at last, the tumultuously beating feminine heart grew still, the living, throbbing being in Richard Dalrymple's arms became a dead weight, and Gwendoline Beattison sank back insensible, a victim to her own uncontrollable emotion.

"Oh, Dick, Dick, where are you? I saw you a minute ago."

Such was the cry—all too late—which, welcome beyond words a few minutes ago, now sounded like the knell of doom in Richard Dalrymple's ears.

Placing Miss Beattison's inanimate form gently against a mossy knoll our perturbed hero presented himself over the wall of foliage and called to his lady-love, "Oh wait there, I will be with you in a minute."

"No, stay where you are," came back the silvery response; "you can't come down, I will cross the river on the stepping stones and come to you."

"Oh, but this is awful," muttered Richard under his breath, "Jeannie will be here in three minutes and will find Miss Beattison, and how on earth can I explain things?"

Then he turned his attention to Miss Beattison, who was slowly regaining consciousness. "Are you feeling better?" he began with a wonderful softness and shamefacedness in eye and tone, when suddenly a piercing scream made him leap to his feet and run to the other side of the bridge.

"My God! Jeannie has fallen in and been swept over the rapids."

Then he sped like a deer across the bridge, down the sloping bank at the further side and past the rushing rapids to the whirling pool where poor Jeannie, still partially buoyed up by her clothes, was whirling around in the grasp of the fatal current.

CHAPTER VII.

A WILD thrill of remorse shot through Richard Dalrymple's heart even as he sprang headlong into the whirlpool, and then he felt as if he was fighting for his life in the embrace of a hundred devil-fish.

This way and that the currents buffeted him, fed in their strength by the momentum of the rapids above, until all the breath was battered out of his body. Suddenly a wayward current threw him against a projecting rock which he caught, thereby probably saving his life. A coward would have ceased his efforts at this point, but not so Richard Dalrymple. Once more the form of his sweetheart met his eye, this time in the pool beyond. Gathering himself up with such strength as he had left, he climbed over the intervening rocks and again plunged to the rescue.

This time his effort was successful. With choking words of encouragement, to cheer his sweetheart, who was fast losing consciousness, by an Herculean effort he swam with her to the lower shore and pushed her gently before him on to the low bank. All at once the friendly swirl of the current changed and he was borne out into the centre of the whirlpool. Again he caught the point of a rock, this time with his feet, and by swimming with all his force, he maintained for a short space a precarious foothold.

He knew that in a very few minutes, his strength being gone, he must cease his efforts and then— —

His brain seemed to become cleared as his strength failed. "Perhaps things are happening for the best," he thought as his arms became like lead, his feet wavered in their hold, and a circling wave caught him in its arms and whirled him off into the lower rapids.

When through the rush of water in his ears he heard a loud cry and his failing sight caught the figure of a woman on horseback dashing in to the foaming current, even in his death throes his heart thrilled as he recognized the form of Miss Beattison.

"Steady, Saladin, steady, now." He heard the ringing tones, he felt a strong touch on his shoulder, and then he was dragged from the foaming water, out of the jaws of death and on to the shelving edge of pebbles which here replaced the jagged rock.

Although considerably bruised by being hurled against the rock by the powerful current, none of Richard Dalrymple's bones were broken and in a few minutes he was able to rise to his feet. He had already been assured by Miss Beattison that Miss Farquharson was reviving. As he rose Miss Beattison was standing by the side of Saladin, who was still panting from his tremendous fight with the current. Saladin's head was between the two, and it seemed at first as if neither cared to round the dangerous point and meet each other after the episode of the bridge.

This time, however, the man was the bolder, and presently Richard Dalrymple stood face to face with Gwendoline Beattison. For an instant her eyes met his with a startled look of conscious shyness, then the downward sweep of the dark lashes veiled their expression, and only the faint color in the cheeks told of the maiden's agitation.

"Miss Beattison, you have saved my life, I thank you for it;" here he raised her hand and gently kissed it; "but indeed I think it would have been better for us all if you had let me drown. Try to forget all that has passed between us to-day, and permit me to assist you to your saddle. I must go to Miss Farquharson's aid."

"Miss Farquharson is in good hands, she is with the gentleman she is about to marry," was the response in a somewhat uneven tone of voice.

"What can you mean, Miss Beattison? Miss Farquharson is engaged to myself."

"To you?" exclaimed the other reining in her horse abruptly. "Oh, the shock of your narrow escape must have then affected your brain,—but look for yourself."

By this time the two had rounded the corner which hid Miss Farquharson from view, and a glance revealed his friend, Alec Douglas, sitting on a boulder with his arm round the waist of Miss Farquharson, whose head lay confidingly on his shoulder.

For a moment, Richard Dalrymple stiffened as if turned into marble, and then arresting the motion of his companion with a wave of his hand he stepped swiftly over the noiseless stretch of sand towards the pair whose backs were towards him.

CHAPTER VIII.

"MY darling," he heard the voice of his friend Alec Douglas saying, "what should I have done if you had been drowned, my bonnie blue-eyed forget-me-not. Who rescued you?"

The grim listener had heard the name of that little flower before, and his lip curled scornfully and bitterly as he heard it now applied by the mouth of another to the woman whom he had always worshipped as his own.

Just for a moment he experienced a passing twinge as a reminder of the scene on the bridge where he had scarcely proven himself the knight without reproach.

But that was only a momentary yielding to a terrible temptation; a man surrenders very little in such an encounter compared with a woman.

Thus he reasoned to himself while his heart told him that such an argument in his case was false, false as the bottomless pit; and that never again in life could he rebuild against that besieger on the bridge, the broken walls and citadel of his heart.

But no man lessens his rage at the defection of another—especially if that other is a woman upon whom he has claims—simply because he happens to be conscious of a like personal frailty; and so, although he staggered under the accusation of his own heart, Richard Dalrymple abated not one whit the contempt of the glance he turned on the unconscious Jeannie.

And beyond all doubt he suffered acutely, although in the tumult of his mind he was conscious of wondering why he did not suffer more. The treachery of his sweetheart shattered an idol on whose worn shrine he had lavished all the love and fealty of his manhood's freshest years, and around which he had twined the fairest garlands which youth's blind unquestioning idolatry can weave.

That the idol he had worshipped was nobler than the divinity it represented, goes without saying where youth's lofty ideal is unchecked and uncorrected by a continual comparison with the original.

Thus poor Jeannie had fallen not only from herself, but she had fallen deeper far from the high ideal her lover had fixed in his mind.

"A badly broken idol," Richard Dalrymple said in looking at Jeannie—and notwithstanding all the ravage done to his own feelings, he was painfully conscious that it was a badly damaged idolater too, who looked on.

"Who rescued you, my darling?" repeated Alec Douglas.

"Oh dear, dear," sobbed his companion, "how can I tell you? the man who saved my life was your friend Richard Dalrymple, and—- and he believes I am engaged to be married to him. Oh, please don't be angry with—me, it was only a girlish love which I have outgrown, and I don't love anyone but you, darling. I had not written to him for months and I thought he would understand that I wished everything to end between us."

To the onlooker the idol seemed more than broken now, it was pulverized to very fine powder indeed.

A heavy shadow falling across the two lovers caused them to turn, and to find themselves face to face with a haggard and dishevelled man, whose pallid face and dark upbraiding eye, caused them to spring hastily to their feet.

Before the image confronting them both found themselves speechless.

"Is that true what you have been saying, Jeannie?" inquired Richard in a hollow voice, "that your love for me was but a girlish fancy, and that you love Douglas here—my old friend Alec, to whom I confided my secret last night?"

No answer save that of downcast eye and burning cheek, and presently a glance of wonderful regret and misery under the long level lashes.

"Betrayed by both betrothed and bosom friend! have *you* nothing to say, Douglas?"

"Yes, indeed, I have, Dalrymple," replied the other; "now, old friend, bear with me awhile. I swear to you I did not know of your engagement until last night—and as far as Jeannie is concerned, she was just telling me that as she had not written you for so long she thought you would understand that she wished to end the engagement. You know," turning softly to Jeannie and laying a gentle caressing hand on her head, "if there is one thing this little girl dreads more than another it is anything approaching a quarrel, and she put off telling you of the change in her feelings thinking that you would scold and make a dreadful upset about it. Of course the whole thing is a terrible mistake all through, but, Dick, I never betrayed a friend in my life, and I would have killed myself rather than have made love to your sweetheart if I had known it."

At this the gentle Jeannie gave a scarcely perceptible toss of her fair head as if to say, "That just shows how much wiser my way was."

"I see, I see," exclaimed the other bitterly, "I have only my own blind unsuspecting devotion to thank for all this. If I had doubted and mistrusted like other men this thing would never have happened. Alec, I bear *you* no malice, you did not know. Jeannie, you made light work of a heart that deserved better from you."

"Oh, Dick, *dear* Dick, please——" began Jeannie, but he waved her away. "Please leave me," he added bitterly, "and if I must do without your love, at least spare me the insult of your pity. Take back your forget-me-nots and broken coin," he added, taking the cigar-case and coin from his pocket and handing them to her still wet with the whirling pool from which he had saved her.

Jeannie would have replied, but the wise Alec, recognizing that much lee-way must be allowed to the disappointed lover, motioned her not to speak, and in silence they left as Richard turned on his heel and strode away across the sand.

When he turned he expected to find himself if not face to face with, at least within reach of, Miss Beattison, and the fact that she was not in sight sent a keen and to him mysterious pang to his heart. He felt he needed the sympathy of someone whose tenderness would not be an insult, and now the only being whom he felt could have poured balm on his wounds had disappeared.

He sat down by the water's edge to think out the new scheme of his life under the altered conditions of the morning, and somehow the tumult of the broken waves seemed a suitable back ground to his thoughts.

For a while he sat in silence revolving the morning's events in his mind, and after a time he drew from his pocket two objects which we, the readers, have seen before.

One was the photograph of Miss Farquharson, and the other the handkerchief found in the train. The former, blurred and defaced by the action of the water in his rescue of Miss Farquharson, caused him to smile a sad, bitter, miserable smile, to which a tear would have been preferable.

"The river ends it all," he said as he tossed the photograph into the torrent, "I almost wish it had ended me too."

Then his eye fell upon the cambric handkerchief found in the train, and a warmth seemed to steal from it, wet and crumpled as it was, which set his heart beating to a faster measure.

"It seems to me," he said softly, "as if all these long years I had been prizing the shell and neglecting the priceless pearl." Then, as he kissed the handkerchief again and again—and now at last without remorse—his mind travelled back to the scene on the bridge. Again in his vision there arose the love illumined eyes and passionate glance of the woman whom he was fain to confess now he had loved fondly even when he fled from her. The passion of her presence seemed again to thrill him as he sat there pressing her handkerchief to his lips, and in the fever of his unrest he sprang to his feet and turned towards the highway, only to find himself face to face with Gwendoline Beattison herself.

For a moment the love-light still burning in his eyes seemed to surprise and dazzle her, and then as he opened wide his arms and murmured the one word "darling," she fled to his heart with a glad cry.

There, eye to eye, heart to heart, and soul to soul, love's dominion was restored, and Cupid's glancing arrows at length found their rightful mark.

THE END.

Lightning Source UK Ltd.
Milton Keynes UK
UKHW050214091019
351185UK00008BA/568/P